LOVE AT ALL RISKS

(Or An Ombudsman's Lot. . .?)

Julian Farrand

Pen Press Publishers Ltd
London

LOVE AT ALL RISKS

(Or An Ombudsman's Lot. . .?)

Julian Farrand

© 2001 Julian Farrand

First Edition

All rights reserved

A catalogue record of this book is available
from the British Library

ISBN1 900796 39 2

Printed and bound in the UK
Published by Pen Press Ltd of London
39-41 North Road, London N7 9DP

Cover Design by
Bridget Tyldsley

A True Story

Only The Material Facts Are False

DEDICATED
To
The Unknown Assistant

AUTHOR'S BIOGRAPHY

Dr Julian Farrand, a solicitor, was appointed Pensions Ombudsman in 1994, after the Maxwell scandal. For 6 years before that he was a controversial Insurance Ombudsman. Whilst a Law Commissioner, in 1984 he chaired the Committee which broke the solicitors' conveyancing monopoly. Previously a Professor of Law at Manchester University, he has become a QC (honorary) and a Fellow of the Chartered Institute of Arbitrators.

Farrand has had numerous legal books and articles published, gained an LL.D (*non*-honorary) from London University. Now, eschewing serious memoirs, he has turned his hand to fiction - the first 'Ombudsman' novel!

CONTENTS

CHAPTER ONE:	Interview Day	1
CHAPTER TWO:	Start Day	21
CHAPTER THREE:	Workadays	38
CHAPTER FOUR:	Witness Day	45
CHAPTER FIVE:	Chequered Day	67
CHAPTER SIX:	Lecture Day	75
CHAPTER SEVEN:	Spag Night	87
CHAPTER EIGHT:	Cases Continued	95
CHAAPTER NINE:	Another Day	110
CHAPTER TEN:	Gloomy Monday	123
CHAPTER ELEVEN:	Nearly Wednesday	135
CHAPTER TWELVE:	Black And Blue Wednesday	154
CHAPTER THIRTEEN:	Wednesday Aftermath	167
CHAPTER FOURTEEN:	Wining Wednesday	170
CHAPTER FIFTEEN:	Wednes-Night	179
CHAPTER SIXTEEN:	Morning After	188
CHAPTER SEVENTEEN:	Friday's Fortune	199
CHAPTER EIGHTEEN:	Fatal Friday	206
CHAPTER NINETEEN:	Weekend Break	213
CHAPTER TWENTY:	Engagement Day	219
CHAPTER TWENTY-ONE:	Last Straw Day	228
CHAPTER TWENTY-TWO:	Penultimate Day	239
CHAPTER TWENTY-THREE:	Final Friday	245

Chapter One

Interview Day

"You are married?" demanded the Chairman, a formidably large lady. Reddish face and square-jawed head under purplish wig-like hair. Dressed in golfer's tweed, her fat, jowls excepted, seemed as firmly held as the contradictory opinions she had imposed throughout the interview. As though cross-examining a hostile witness, she had put a series of leading questions - on education (single-sex schools vital for our gels, but mixed essential for the lads), employment (married women make better managers than men, but wives and mothers should be stay-at-home-makers), government (less taxation and regulation, but more expenditure on hospitals and the army), agriculture (farmers are profiteers), gardening (flower arrangers should grow their own) and other intellectual or recreational pursuits (theatre is elevating but cinema full of foreign filth whilst golf is good, football bad). All called for simple and, for preference, silent assent; none appeared remotely relevant to the appointment.

The Ombudsman winced. Sitting beside and slightly behind the Chairman at the far end of a long table, he had not yet attempted to ask or even say anything, but he had grimaced frequently, shaking his head with tight-closed eyes as if in pain, whilst smirking occasionally, nodding his head and trying to twinkle his eyes as if in

1

fun. He had, however, worn a very warm greeting grin and had also smiled encouragingly at the candidate during the traditional CV recital with which the interview had opened.

How dare she ask that? thought Charlotte (Lottie to her family and friends but Lot to significant others). A solicitor by qualification and experience, she was well aware that sexually-discriminating questions ought to be avoided at job interviews: disappointed candidates might sue. But that was not what bothered her. She had already explained, plausibly perhaps, that after ten years profitable practice as a personal injuries litigator she had taken an extended career break to bear and bring up twin babies. Daniel and Benjamin had proved to be hyperactive boys, far too demanding and exhausting to permit of any return to work. Hitherto, at any rate.

In fact, conception had been a unilateral decision on her part which had upset her husband extraordinarily. Gynaecologist to the wealthy, he had not only abandoned the twins' care and nurture entirely to her, but had also ceased to see her as a stimulating specimen and discontinued intercourse. At least with her: on Christmas Eve she had caught him continuing with his surgery nurse.

Contrite apparently, blaming seasonal goodwill and professing love past and present plus fidelity for the future, he had fully financed a live-in nanny for the twins, now 3-year-old terrorists, and restored intercourse with her on Saturday mornings. Nevertheless, she had not enjoyed the first instalment of this dutiful weekly act, believed he had not either and feared their marriage

Chapter One

to be entering a terminal decline. Her mother, twice divorced but now a wealthy widow residing alone in Islington, continued to urge the attractions of divorce - she had found her own enjoyable as well as rewarding - and offered comfortable accommodation for her daughter and, of course, the grandtwins at the top of her tall terrace house. She had not explicitly encouraged widowhood although mentioning that there might be money in it.

However, Charlotte believed that her mother desired the presence not so much of her daughter as of her beloved grandsons and feared that her desire might not survive the permanent reality. The precious peace and order of life in a secluded square of gentrified gothic-style dwellings could quickly be shattered by the sounds, smells and foot or fisticuffs of tiny terrorists. Nor did she want to start listening to her mother's advice at this mature stage in her life: she had married Simon mainly, she remembered, as a means of escape - and against maternal advice. Nevertheless, in anxious anticipation of the marriage's dissolution and in pursuance of her perennial New Year's Resolution, she was taking a first tentative step towards restarting her broken career and stalled brain. However none of this was any business whatsoever of the Chairman.

"I have a spouse legally in place, but why do you ask?" Charlotte replied with a big cat's smile. Short brownish hair and big greenish eyes, with high cheekbones and a tiny chin, created a distinctly feline face which at rest seemed serious and somewhat sombre. This impression was not really misleading for emotion made her cry: one of the nuns at her convent school had said to her parents when she was three: "Lottie's a very tragic child." Yet she could as readily weep at happiness, her own or other people's. And her face was rarely seen at rest. Rather it was constantly if unconsciously reflecting the reactions, feelings, needs and observations of an uncommonly energetic intelligence. She was as likely to flash with laughter as flush with tears. But she could still cry for England.

"Ah! Good," said the Chairman. "We like to know the whole person."

The impossibility of achieving this through an interview, especially one she had conducted, showed no sign of troubling her. However, a Thatcherite handbag rested within reach on the table and she put one hand on it - defensively or threateningly, Charlotte could not be sure.

The Ombudsman winked. "Well," he said standing up, "thank you very much Lady Cocks, but we mustn't keep you any longer from more important matters. The MD is sure to want a word with you."

Did the Chairman's cheeks dimple and pinken ever so slightly?

"I'll talk Mrs Davies through the boring details of the work before handing her over to Robin to complete the documentation," added the Ombudsman ushering Charlotte out of the Council Chamber.

"A choice addition to your bevy of beauties, Oliver?" called Lady Cocks after them.

The Ombudsman turned back. "Now, now Chairman - positive discrimination is not in itself a sin."

CHAPTER ONE

Charlotte Davies, *née* - nearly 38 years ago - Angus, a surname she definitely intended to readopt as Ms, followed the Ombudsman down a dog-legged corridor cluttered with cabinets bursting with clumsy files. A couple of inches or so shorter than her, despite the non-threateningly low heels sensibly chosen by the taller than average female for such occasions, he was stocky to the point of portliness, a plumpish impression accentuated by the green corduroy suit plus waistcoat and watch chain he had, less sensibly perhaps, seen fit to wear. Greyish curly hair, fierce glasses on a snub nose and prominent ears, together with the grimacing and smirking throughout the interview, had projected a disconcertingly impish image. She knew from the papers sent with the interview invitation that Oliver Goodman had for a long time been a Professor of Law at a minor provincial university before becoming Ombudsman nearly two years earlier when he was 50 and the scheme was launched by the British Insurance Group Ltd.

The BIG insurer was how it liked to be known: "BIG is better" ran its adverts "especially for little people," picturing Snow White advising the seven dwarfs to seek protection against various inventively devastating risks. The recommended protector was not a charming prince but a genial giant, peculiarly called "BIG policy!" Snow White's commission was not disclosed but was rumoured to include free cover against food poisoning, with infections caused by princely kisses costing extra. At the beginning of 1987 BIG had announced "an exciting new concept in consumer protection: instead of being judge and jury in handling claims, BIG has established an independent Ombudsman to investigate policyholders' complaints." He had opened his doors for business on April Fools' Day.

Strictly speaking, as Charlotte the lawyer appreciated, the accusation against insurance companies was that they were prosecutor and judge, since it is perfectly normal for judges to act, in effect, as juries as well in non-criminal cases. That meant prosecutor in the sense of charging their own policyholders with the felony of faking claims. Be that as it may, the Ombudsman's decisions would bind BIG up to £100,000.

Now, according to the notice Charlotte had spotted in *The Times* one Tuesday, an extra "Technical Assistant" to the Ombudsman was required to cope with the aftermath of storms and Stock Exchange crash in October 1987. Evidently BIG had not accepted all claims of damage and complaints misselling as undeniably valid. Consumerist criticism was quite misconceived: if flat-felt roofs had been kept properly repaired they would not have blown off, Lady Cocks had explained with righteous indignation, and greedy investors deserved no sympathy whatsoever. Her fellow interviewer had looked particularly pained at this and shaken his head excessively, but whether in support or not neither Charlotte nor, happily, the Chairman could be sure.

At the end of the corridor they arrived at an open door. "For pushing at," said the Ombudsman. The door bore no apparent indication of the empty room's

CHAPTER ONE

expected occupancy, although there was a doormat bearing the legend: 'NOT UNWELCOME.' Charlotte rightly supposed it was his room, as he gestured her inside.

"Coffee?" he asked. "How do you like it?"

"Black, no sugar, thank you."

"Me too, I'll fetch some, go on in, back soon." He hurried away down the corridor.

The Ombudsman's office, not unlike himself, was comparatively compact but oddly shaped - an irregularly-sided oblong with two turret windows. The views, over Bloomsbury Square and Sicilian Avenue, might prove distractingly attractive, thought Charlotte, as could the smell of the Spaghetti House below. Law books, on DIY shelving, concealed the walls. Glancing at the titles, she saw they were almost all texts about property law. Indeed only two were obviously about insurance at all: a big hardback by Hardy-Ivamy and a small softback by Birds - the former, unlike the latter, was dog-eared and the latter, unlike the former, was dust-free.

Charlotte sat down on the typist's chair in front of the Ombudsman's desk. That was too large for the room and completely covered by files and piles of paper. She waited a while, wondering whether the piles were orderly. Eventually he returned carrying two cups carefully.

"Sorry about the wait, had to brew some more. My fault, should have warned her."

Who? she wondered, but only said, "Does all this mean that I've got the job?"

Oliver laughed. "With your qualifications, you'd get

it even if you were a chap! The other Assistants, all three of them, good girls - sexist of me, but I only do it to annoy - you'll soon find they're neither good nor girls," he hastily interrupted himself. Charlotte's expression must have revealed her reaction.

"Anyway they all come from insurance or consumerist backgrounds. I desperately need another lawyer to talk to and one that got a good upper second, if only from Cambridge, and has also had ten years experience in practice should do me very well. That interview was just to humour the Chairman, she is supposed to approve all appointments and she'd only get upset if I left her out of the process. Injured pride, you know. The real question is whether you still want the job now that you've met Lady Cocks."

Not to mention you, thought Charlotte.

"Incidentally," he added. "I take it that your personal injuries litigation did involve insurance companies?"

"Oh yes, all the time," she replied. "Acting for and against, but always behind defendants - they've quite a taste for fighting actions in the courts so long as they're not named as parties, no bad publicity - good clients, but BIG was not one of them so I'm not tainted, if that's what you're asking."

"Excellent," said the Ombudsman. "There's a well known judicial tendency to be prejudiced against former clients - you know, leaning over backwards to do justice, or doing them down to show absence of bias, which may only mean that the judge knew his old client well enough to distrust him or it properly. I wouldn't want us to be accused of that sort of thing - we're subjected

CHAPTER ONE

to too much ill-founded criticism as it is."

Full membership of the pompous tendency, Charlotte speculated.

"From the job title, presumably we work in laboratories," was all she remarked.

"What? Oh, I see. No 'technical' is just an insurance industry euphemism for anything remotely complicated - you can call yourself 'legal assistant' if you like, or even 'solicitor' for all I care, after all you are one and the punters may be impressed. But I doubt if BIG'll be willing to buy you a practising certificate," said Oliver.

"They pay a pittance for the privilege of working here," he continued, "because BIG sets salaries at the lowest equivalent insurance industry levels. Fortunately for me, this is significantly higher than a professorial stipend, but it can't compete, of course, with the pecuniary perks of legal practice. So recruitment is a problem. In fact, you were a shortlist of one."

Charlotte thought she might only stay until a better offer arrived and then there would be none, but ventured a question: "Why does BIG pay so little?"

Oliver sighed. "Cynically speaking, the scheme was never an altruistic and generous gesture but a PR and marketing stunt to be played on a shoestring. In the mid-80s the insurance industry became seriously threatened with statutory rules and regulation. Politicians appeared on the point of giving the punters, sorry personal policyholders, a fair deal of all things. So defensive options were considered by the insurers' trade association. Favourite was 'self-governance' via the association - rather like solicitors and The Law Society, hardly a persuasive precedent for the consumer lobby. 'Do nothing' had a following whilst many insurance lawyers understandably advocated binding arbitration arrangements. But BIG's Bob pulled a fast one."

"Who?" interjected Charlotte, realising belatedly that she had triggered-off a former university lecturer (traditionally 50 minutes worth of words) and trying to divert the flow.

"Robert Walker, BIG's Managing Director," was the answer. "Looks like a bald Henry VIII in a pin-stripe suit. He'd been to some Scandinavian conference and heard about their Ombudsmen. His brainwave had two angles. First, BIG policies could gain a marketing advantage by being sold with a built-in Ombudsman option. Second, he genuinely believed, along with the rest of the industry, that there really were no justifiable complaints against insurers, either generally or BIG in particular. So an Ombudsman would have nothing to do except explain to punters that BIG had handled their claim correctly. Then after a couple of years, having demonstrated economically that government interference was unnecessary, the scheme could be quietly terminated."

"Obviously that part of his brainwave hasn't worked," said Charlotte.

"No, unhappily for him, our new business has blossomed, even if his hasn't. From part-time and single-handed, I've grown to full-time and three now four expert assistants. Happily for us, the scheme can't simply be scrapped like any other over-budget advertising campaign, partly because of the poor publicity for BIG and the risk of legislation, but mainly because of loss of face for BIG's Bob. Chief executives of insurance companies may look like burly bruisers and behave like feudal lords, but underneath they are all sensitive, insecure creatures!"

"But if it is BIG's scheme and it pays the bills, especially if it does so out of its advertising budget, how can you pretend to be independent?" questioned Charlotte, in a deliberate attempt to upset the Ombudsman.

"Easy!" said he, not that easily upset. "To appease the National Consumer Council, the scheme incorporated a buffer Council between BIG and Ombudsman. With only two BIG nominees outnumbered by four of the not very great or good, led by Lady Cocks, Council appoints and, hopefully, reappoints Ombudsmen. So I can certainly say I'm independent of BIG so far as job security goes."

"But surely you are still dependent and insecure in that BIG could cut funding and close you down whenever it alone wanted to, "said Charlotte, still trying to annoy.

"Correct," conceded Oliver quietly, looking annoyed. "And, almost worse, my constitutional accountability to Council produces, in practice, a different depth of dependence. It's not just the fact that Council members receive fees from BIG, substantial in the Chairman's case pro rata she is paid more than I am - that bothers me. What really gets up my nose," he was becoming less academic, that is, for anyone unfamiliar with academics, "is Council's conceit that the scheme was created for their benefit, to confer centre-stage significance on them with their opinions rather than mine being of public importance. They behave as if their primary rôle is to keep the Ombudsman in his place." He actually snorted.

"The Chairman herself was a schoolteacher, before she caught her poor old Peer of a husband, and now acts as if she's Headmistress and I'm, at best, head boy. On top of this, she has some sort of dalliance going on with BIG's Bob - you know, the MD I said wanted a word. He's even larger than she is and makes her feel like a little girl again - calls her 'our Jenny'. No one believes it's anything more than platonic flirting - he is a widower but the very thought of those two physically coupling always self-distructs. But it's useful to him, if he doesn't like what I'm doing or, more likely, saying to the Press, he rings her ladyship up and she has me on her carpet, so to speak. All this encourages me to be extremely bloody-minded, even if I'm not actually independent, which may not be a bad thing, according on your point of view."

"What's the view-point of the rest of Council?" Charlotte asked, feeling a little deafened by the noise of personalities clashing, if not also egos breaking.

"Well, the two BIG nominees have always been totally opposed to their MD's idea, but Bob's not a man who tolerates opposition gladly so they content themselves with more or less polite hostility. You'll have a lot to do with them because they handle the cases coming to the office. Richard Scott is their Claims Manager for general insurance policies, he's an old-

CHAPTER ONE

timer who relies on his 'nose' to tell him which claims are valid and otherwise assumes claimants to be fraudulent until proven innocent. Trouble is his nose often turns out to be right. The other is Kevin Lightman - Life and Finance Director, head-hunted for BIG from a firm of accountants as Bob's successor. He'd found accountancy too exciting, so got some actuarial qualifications. That was five or six years ago and Bob's not gone yet: so his heir apparent is getting a bit bitter. He's no feel for insurance ethics and is only interested in company profits - for the shareholders not the policyholders. They like to be called "Scotty" and "Mr Lightman" but behind their backs they're known by everybody as "Arms" and "Fingers" - you'll find out why from the girls, something to do with their 'hands-on' approach to staff and money, I believe."

"And the non-BIG Council members?" she sought to stem the slanders, but only offered a different target.

"Useless but harmful," Oliver replied, the gestures with which he was speaking becoming expressively dismissive.

"They don't know enough about insurance to argue with the BIG nominees," he continued, "and so out of committee cronyism lend silent support to their criticisms of me. On top of this, one or two of them harbour ambitions to be listed as 'greater and gooder' merely by virtue of being on this Council. Apart from the Chairman, there's Hughie Laddie, a freelance consumer consultant whose line is communication. 'If I cannot understand your decision, how can the poor policyholder possibly be expected to?' he declaims.

Because, unlike you, he's not necessarily stupid, I never say, though I do waffle on about not under-estimating the average mental ages of the insured population - he doesn't catch on. Then there's Bill Blackburne, a Polytechnic economist, who always questions the implications for the EEC - there never are any - and even for the world on a micro-scale, all this demonstrating the depths of polyintellect."

Is this elitism or just a little contemptuous? wondered Charlotte.

"He spots typos in our letters, points them out with pride - I'm always very grateful. Last and least comes little Frankie Freeman. The Chairman co-opted her out of nowhere. They'd met at a tea-party for ladies who play games - golf or tennis, that means. She's a small woman who was something small in the Girl Guides' movement - at headquarters, not camping. Diploma in Business Studies at Bristol College of Commerce."

His contempt was now tangible and Charlotte thought still excessively elitist.

"Wears wide shoulders and flares her nostrils. Completely out of her depth, speaks a lot in an unfamiliar language - management jargon - though, to be fair, she does at least sometimes say we should decide more cases in favour of complainants, never mind the merits, to give the scheme credibility with organised consumerists."

"But aren't you notoriously known as the Consumers' Champion?" Charlotte asked, trying to see where he stood apart from his manifestly unsafe estimates of

Chapter One

everyone else he had mentioned.

"True but, of course, it's extremely upsetting," he said, looking pleased, "and factually untrue. I decide in BIG's favour 70% of the time but insurers like Arms and Fingers think I'm biased against them because its not 100%. Then the media make it worse by giving over-the-top publicity to complainants who do succeed. Not good advertising! But it's not my rôle to champion anyone - I'm supposed to be an independent adjudicator deciding each case impartially. In the real world, of course, no-one at all wants this - people prefer me to be completely partial to their side."

"Is BIG good then, winning such a high percentage?" she wondered aloud.

"BIG's not bad. The problem to begin with is that policyholders have exaggerated expectations - not their fault, the insurance industry goes in for very positive selling, not just BIG's sickening Snow White commercial but campaigns like 'We won't make a drama out of a crisis' and 'Get the strength of insurance round you'. The consequence is that any negative claims-handling comes as a nasty surprise and complaints are made to me about reliance on small print in cases when no-one in their right-mind should think they're actually covered."

"However, there's another less obvious aspect. When the scheme was set up BIG restricted the Ombudsman's Terms of Reference so as to exclude the things people mostly complain about."

"What are those?" asked Charlotte, although by now rather bored.

"Premium levels, third-party claims, small businesses, underwriting decisions excluding individuals or occupations or inner-city areas from cover. A pretty example occurs with life insurance policies. Originally these were going to be left out of the scheme altogether as too straightforward to give rise to any disputes and were only included so as to 'extend the educational scope of the service' by letting the Ombudsman explain why surrender values were nil for the first few years. However, the Terms of Reference then specifically excluded surrender values and other actuarial matters from my jurisdiction, in order to avoid any risk of price-sensitive interference! So we are actually not allowed to give any educational explanations, even if we wanted to, whilst, in fact, we do get lots of other complaints concerning life policies."

"To do with doubtful deaths, I suppose," said Charlotte.

"We do get a few of those," replied Oliver, "but I meant the financial advice side. Indeed this is a growth area following the stock-exchange crash in 1987 - the commonest complaint is that investment-linked policies were sold on the basis that they would never go down in value, 'safe as houses' it was always said, but they had gone down. 'Only a blip,' says Fingers, 'and our reps would always warn that investments can go down as well as up.' He's probably right about the blip but I rarely believe that reps on commission give any audible warnings, so I usually set the sale aside - to the likely long-term disadvantage of the punter."

"But enough of background," said the Ombudsman

Chapter One

suddenly, pulling out his pocket-watch. Evidently the 50 minutes were expiring.

"The mechanics of what you will do as an Assistant should be dead easy. You take a file from the bottom of the pile - that means the oldest complaint in the backlog cabinets in the corridor - Robin thinks 'stockpile' sounds better than 'backlog' - actually you should take half-a-dozen or so to work on. Then you read the complaint and the correspondence with BIG, consider any reports - loss adjuster's, doctor's, engineer's or whatever - and ask questions seeking further information as you think necessary. Lastly you draft a decision letter for me to sign. Occasionally, of course, I read the letters before signing them, and then you may have to put up with me amending or even rejecting them."

"On what basis should decisions be reached?" Charlotte cautiously enquired.

"According to law and a proper construction of the policy," replied the Ombudsman, "but only if that's in favour of the policyholder. Usually it isn't - in the past insurance law has been deliberately bent by the courts in favour of insurers in shipping and commercial cases in ways most lawyers even agree is not justifiable for personal insurance."

I know, I know, she thought.

"So then you have to ask yourself: is this fair and reasonable? If not, decide differently. Difficult for a lawyer - means thinking like the man on the Clapham Omnibus, or woman on the Clapham underground, eh? ha!"

Not funny, not bloody funny, she thought,

17

contemplating commuting again.

"I sometimes liken my rôle, rather pretentiously you may think, to that of medieval Chancellors who were supposed to be 'The Keeper of the King's Conscience' - the problem is finding the conscience of an insurance company in the first place!"

Definitely pretentious, thought Charlotte.

"If in doubt, come and ask - I operate an open-door policy," he said.

At which a hatchet-face poked in through the open door, and said: "Don't forget your lunch-time appointment, Professor Goodman."

"Thank you, Mrs Arden, nearly finished. Any questions, Mrs Davies?"

"Yes, a couple," she said, deciding to postpone the Ms Angus idea. "First do Assistants make site visits and interview witnesses and such like?"

"Not often, in fact hardly ever," replied the professor. "Almost all decisions are made 'off the papers' by deskbound investigators. If anything or anyone needs examining, we instruct consultant experts to do it for us. However, you will be bombarded with telephone calls and sometimes I hold oral hearings to test credibility - very informal, lawyers discouraged - no costs awarded, just the complainant plus Arms or Fingers up from head-office in Bournemouth and any witnesses, usually only a protesting salesman, with me asking the questions. Breaks the monotony! What's your other question?"

"When do you want me to start?" was all she could still bear to ask, for fear of a further lecture.

Chapter One

"ASAP," said he. "What about next Wednesday, February 1st - complete months, more convenient you know."

"Top of the salary range?" she pushed - at an open door.

"Naturally, and there are even pension arrangements: BIG will let you buy one of its personal pensions and not ungenerously contribute up to 5% itself whilst also waiving a not completely negligible part of its own charges."

Was this sarcasm heavy enough? both wondered.

"Alright, next Wednesday it is," said she, contemplating very early retirement, never mind the pension.

"Very good, I'm really glad," the Ombudsman replied, rubbing his hands together. "Now go and see the office boy. . ." Who? she felt like asking, but thought better of it. "He'll deal with all the employment details. But you will have to excuse me, I have an appointment now. Mrs Arden will take you along to him."

Hatchet-face re-appeared round the door attached to a steely-permed head on a bony body, an ancient but far from feeble lady - pinkish twin-set, tartan skirt, flat shoes.

"Ah, Mrs Arden, would you be so kind as to show Mrs Davies where to find Mr Wood. See you on the 1st then!"

Hatchet-face said "This way" to Charlotte, who felt she had missed another Ms Angus opportunity, and "You can go in now," to three figures skulking outside, only one of them female. As Charlotte stood to leave,

19

wondering still about the 'office-boy', she thought she saw the Ombudsman taking two packs of cards from a desk-drawer. Obediently, she followed Mrs Arden's ram-rod back, marching in step, retracing the route along the cluttered corridor towards the Council Chamber until they reached a closed door bearing a sign:

GENERAL MANAGER
AND
CLERK TO COUNCIL

Hatchet-face knocked perfunctorily and entered immediately. Inside a larger room than the Ombudsman's, behind a larger desk, sat a weedy thirtyish male playing with his toys. No papers sullied the desk-top. His face was boyish despite a jet-black, triple-Hitler moustache and toupée-style hair. He smiled with annoyance at Mrs Arden as she left, then leered amateurishly at Charlotte:
"Do you like soldiers?"
She looked non-plussed and negative whilst noticing what his toys were. He carefully cleared the toy soldiers into a drawer and took out a file labelled in bold italics: *'Charlotte Davies, Mrs.'* She contemplated mentioning the Ms Angus issue, but the moment seemed unpropitious.
"So what sort of men do you like?" he continued, still leering.
Not your sort, you office toy-boy, she thought, whilst affecting a chuckle through lightly-gritted teeth.

Chapter Two

Start Day

Quite early but not very brightly on February the 1st 1989, Charlotte crossed all the roads from Holborn Tube station and climbed the stairs to the second-floor offices of the BIG Insurance Ombudsman Scheme. She was well-wrapped, against the cold, coat over trouser-suit, scarf over stiff upper lip - this being a reaction against apprehension. The twins had been far too busy fighting to notice, never mind grieve, her departure but Nanny Rosa had looked relieved as she waved her off. Her once-beloved spouse must have left even earlier in the Jag. That is if he had ever come home - she had slept in the spare bedroom to be sure of a snore-free night before the BIG day. She had quite forgotten the underground Hell of packed commuters. The Holborn traffic and congested pavements were another reminder of bad times past. Was it worth it? She sought an escape from domestic disharmony but already wanted to escape from the escape. Yet perhaps the work would prove rewarding, although hardly financially, and her new colleagues similarly stimulating. . . or perhaps not.

The BIG O's office-door was glazed and locked, by combination not key. She rang the doorbell and saw a Marilyn Monroe look-alike hopeful, but her figure a bit under-featured for that purpose, sitting at a reception desk. The receptionist, if such she was, turned towards her, still talking into a telephone and staying seated.

Charlotte shouted "I'm expected" and rang again, for longer.

Blondie waved to her without otherwise moving. Charlotte started to beat on the glass door with the flat of her hand. Blondie waved her away. Just as fists flew glasswards, Robin Wood opened the door, at some personal risk. He was wearing a lapel badge: 'General Manager'. She learnt that once a month he wore the same leer but another badge: 'Clerk to Council'.

"Sorry about that - Sarah's social life does, of course, take priority over her office duties," he leered menacingly, disconnecting the phone.

"Sarah, let me introduce Mrs Davies, our new Technical Assistant, a solicitor of the acceptable sort."

"Hey, I hadn't finished my call," Blondie snarled at him, before simpering at her.

"Awfully sorry, I thought you were a policyholder. We don't let them in - they're always complaining, you know. I need to be told before they come that there's an appointment and someone's going to meet them. Otherwise for all I care, they can just wait outside."

"Sarah Potts, Mrs Arden's handicap, she'd sooner let a horse in than an unknown woman - men she doesn't let out!" leered the office-boy.

Charlotte had begun to appreciate the Ombudsman's reference to his manager. She discovered later that Sarah was actually a very accomplished rider, jumps and dressage (on well-trained horses, bumps and undressage on trainee boy-friends) as well as quite accomplished at typing (sic) decision letters. She had also missed one more opportunity of asking for Angus

Chapter Two

as a surname:

"Hello, call me Lottie, short for Charlotte, and let me in next time," was all she said.

"Oh! Hi, no problem, but anyway the door-lock code is 1-2-3-4, too obvious for burglars and easy enough for Lady Cocks to remember, Robbie always says!"

The General Manager hastily led Charlotte away from the reception area towards the Council Chamber where she had been interviewed. Without knocking he opened the door a crack and sang out:

"No longer little Miss Lonely."

"Bugger off!" shouted the occupant.

Sniggering to himself and without hesitation, Robin, the manager-man entered. Charlotte followed, not without hesitation although not exactly expecting to encounter Lady Cocks again, which she did not. Instead she saw a little girl with curly red hair topping a round white but red-lipped face and wearing red leggings who was doing a comical hopping dance. Then she realised that this was really a young woman simulating extreme fury.

"Your new room-mate," announced the Robin. "Mrs Davies meet Madeleine Hill. I'm afraid you two will have to share the table until desks are sorted out. Maddie," leering, "you will show Charlotte the ropes, won't you?"

"Piss off," she replied and he did.

"Marian will never get desks organised, the useless pratt," said Maddie.

"Marian?"

"Oh, that's just what he's called. Not Robin Hood

but Maid Marian - you know -

> 'Robin Wood, Robin Wood,
> With his band of Men,
> Riding through the Gym
> On his sturdy Glen. . .'

He goes to the YMCA, no wife, no girl friend that anyone knows of, plays with toy soldiers, so everyone thinks he's gay really, despite all his suggestive leering. But who knows? Come on, hang your coat up and have a cup of coffee."

Charlotte noticed and smelt an electric filter-coffee machine on the go.

"Yes please," she said. "I'm Charlotte but Lottie for short."

"OK Lottie it is," said the other, "and as you'll have guessed I'm called Maddie - name and nature, etc. etc. We know you're a really brilliant lawyer because the Prof's been boasting about catching you."

"The Prof?" queried Charlotte, knowing the answer.

"Ollie the Ombudsman, that's what he's usually called, short for Professor Goodman, sir, and he likes it, reminds him of his intellectual credentials. He'll be here any moment now for coffee and a chat-up."

"Doesn't his secretary make him coffee?" asked Charlotte, not knowing the answer.

"He's not allowed to have his own secretary, Council think he might do personal things and get above himself. No, old Hard-on is the Scheme's 'secretarial service', types for all of us, helped or hindered by tarty Sarah, of course. Her first name's Mary, but nobody calls her anything except Mrs Arden - except behind her back, of course. She used to be BIG's Bob's personal assistant, reached retirement age then a couple of years later her husband couldn't stand the strain and pegged out. Bob gave her this job, probably so she could spy on the Prof. But, old as she is, she's very, very efficient. More than can be said for Marian - or Sarah!"

At this point, the door flung open - does nobody knock, wondered Charlotte - and, sure enough, the Ombudsman arrived. Wearing a light grey cloth suit, no waistcoat, red tie, he was looking a little less portly.

"Ah, here you are," he said. So perceptive, she thought.

"And you've met Maddie," he added proving conclusively, she accepted, that professorial perceptions were not unperceptive.

"She's my oldest Assistant, you know - sorry longest-standing, first, senior," he corrected in response to a drop dead look from the young woman in question. "Knows more about what we do than anyone, even me."

"Especially you," Charlotte heard Maddie mutter. But the Ombudsman was helping himself to coffee.

"Have you met Chip and Mount?"

She shook her head, wondering who or what.

"Let's do the introductions now. Maddie can tell you what to do later."

All three trooped out into the corridor, carefully carrying cups of coffee. Past Sarah at reception on the phone, turning right down a short passage, they reached an unmarked door. The Ombudsman threw it open, no knocking. The two occupants sat back-to-back at typist's desks littered with papers from open files. They were holding dictaphones at the ready. The room was small, no books, one window, no pictures but a cork board above each desk pinned all over with notices, memos, photos, press cuttings and cartoons. Heaps of files surrounded the desks and the air was blue. As they entered, one of the occupants scrabbled in a drawer which she slammed shut.

"Council insists on a strict no smoking policy for the office, scrupulously observed, of course," said the Ombudsman.

Charlotte could now see that none of his 'good girls' was actually a girl. They were all women and Maddie was easily the youngest.

"Cilla, Veronica, meet Charlotte Davies at long last."

Cilla McCarthy, tiny wiry mid-forties, wearing jeans and a jumper, with a bright lively chipmunk face was plainly 'Chip'. Originally from Liverpool, her maiden name was White - and she did not owe her first name to parental wit, although subsequent references to the locally grown pop star, Cilla Black, suggesting some sort of witticism, rarely led to denials. She had researched for *Which?*, where she was equally wittily called 'Killer', specialising in second-hand car scams until meeting and marrying a second-hand car dealer. After this she had concentrated on car insurance scams whilst bearing him no fewer than five children in as many years. Not Roman Catholics, just careless contraceptors. She still self-selected from the backlog

CHAPTER TWO

any car cases: they mostly concerned the market-value of written-off vehicles: 'pristine condition, well-maintained, top of the price range,' pleaded the punter; 'rusty rubbish, accident damage, outside Glass's Guide, ex gratia token sum,' insisted Arms. Maddie had re-nicknamed her Chip, which had stuck even with her husband who now enjoyed a nice little earner on the side as the Ombudsman's car consultant. She kept a desk-drawer clear for stubbing-out fag-ends - a disgusting fire-risk, tolerated by her colleagues more for the sake of a quiet life than out of unsought sympathy for her pressurised non-life style.

Veronica Mountford was vast: six foot two and built like an unfit second-row forward, sumo wrestling came to mind, long grey-lank-hair around a jolly scrubbed fat-face, she was in her early fifties. Bought her clothes from OXFAM, or so it appeared to Charlotte. One clever child still studying, post-graduate geography, her husband a life-long life insurance salesman dependent on commission but much too conscientious for his own good or his family's finances. They had met whilst she too had worked in-house for one of the so-called Scottish Mafia, life companies with headquarters huddling together in Edinburgh. So she would seize upon any backlog complaints concerning life insurance - or rather assurance, as if this were possible - and judge them by her own and her spouse's high standards. Her weakness was an inherent inability to see anything through the eyes of a non-insurance person, coupled with a firm faith that everyone should be sold life cover, preferably linked with investments, in their own very best interests whether they knew they wanted it or not. Misselling complaints caused her severe problems in principle but if the salesman had failed to follow her book of acceptable sales practices (pre-LAUTRO, unpublished) she would be merciless. Three falls and a submission were as nothing. Even before taking her married name, 'woman mountain', shortened to 'Mount', was an apt nickname still sticking.

The 'girls', a spectacularly mis-matched pair, leapt from their seats to welcome Charlotte with exaggerated enthusiasm. One looking down, the other up, they seized her hands and shook them vigorously whilst uttering an extraordinary duet:

"We're so glad" -

"you've joined us."

Truly? Charlotte doubted.

"The Prof has been telling everyone all about you" -

"being such a brilliant lawyer."

Fallen on hard times! thought Charlotte.

"How lucky we should feel" -

"you'll be able to help us with all our difficult cases."

And into bad company? Charlotte wondered.

"Now, now, you two," the Ombudsman intervened, "you're overdoing it. Charlotte may well take a day or two to get completely on top of the work."

Shut up, she screamed silently, retrieving her hands and saying, entirely tactfully: "Hi Mount, Lo Chip! My friends usually call me Lottie, I do hope we'll be friends and, look, I know I'll need the rest of you to explain what's going on for ages."

"As it happens," the Ombudsman continued not

CHAPTER TWO

entirely tactfully, "I did suggest that anything with a legal element ought to be left in the backlog cupboard for you to deal with, so you might find your first batch quite interesting and I'm sure the others will want to consult you all the time."

At which he departed hastily, no doubt in the interests of health and safety, his own.

Happily 'the girls' ignored the Ombudsman and took no other offence.

"Well Lottie, don't ask Maddie for any explanations, that's all," said Chip.

"She'll give them anyway," said Mount.

"And you won't like them," added Chip.

"They'll be wrong!" added Mount.

"Shut your faces, you dozy old cows," Maddie riposted humorously, at least the peculiar pair were laughing at her. "Actually, I have selected a dozen or so files from the cupboard for you - they're piled on the table in our room - and, surprise surprise, some of them do seem to be rejects from our intellectually challenged colleagues here."

They tittered together.

"Come on Lottie, you'll see more than enough of them." Charlotte turned to go, saying:

"See you then," over her shoulder as the odd couple intoned:

"Don't look back, Lot," -

"pass the salt to-morrow!"

Not that joke again, she thought.

As they exited, the General Manager badge emerged from its room.

"A word if you please, Mrs Davies. I'll send her along in just a moment, Maddie."

Still carrying her half empty, wholly cold coffee cup, Charlotte reluctantly but compliantly went once again into his room and sat down unasked, although not unremarked - lips pursed. She observed, as before, a presence of filing cabinets and an absence of books, but this time also one lone large picture on the walls: Her Gracious Majesty, the Queen, inspecting the Guard of Honour. Pretty soldiers!

"It occurred to me that you might be under the impression that the Ombudsman runs things in the office. Actually, as General Manager, of course, I'm in charge. Technical Assistants are accountable to me. Please don't forget that and remember that you're strictly on six months' probation."

So are you, she thought, if that long.

"Let me assure you that I have the Chairman's ear."

Whilst the Ombudsman only has her tongue on the carpet, so to speak, I get the message, Charlotte thought sourly, but only said sweetly:

"There is something I'm sure only you could do for me."

"Yes, yes," he leered, "anything within reason, Lottie, if I may so call you."

This trip only, you're not a friend, but:

"I really would like to use my maiden name again, to mark my new employment status you know, so could I please be known in the office, if it's not too much trouble, as Ms Angus?"

Ms Angus returned to the Council Chamber content

CHAPTER TWO

at re-achieving her nominal maidenhood, albeit at the cost of token mutterings and leering implications. Maddie looked up from her paperwork:

"Marian the Manager's in charge?"

"Right," nodded Charlotte.

"Don't you believe it - the Prof doesn't get involved in any admin if he can avoid it but likes to keep his girls happy and hates petty bureaucracy. Take a problem to him and Marian caves in - he'll whinge to Cocksey, but neither of them want Council to know they can't actually control the Ombudsman."

Charlotte only said: "Do you mind if I take another coffee? I'm exhausted already."

"Help yourself. I have a half and half kitty with the Prof - we'll make it thirds if that's OK - though he gets more than his fair share most days, as well as his droit de chat-up, as he calls it. And don't let the terrible two get on top of you in any sense. They'll get used to you. Their double act is worse than their fight."

What on earth does she mean? wondered Charlotte.

"What about the Prof - will he be a problem?" she asked.

"Not unless you fall in love with him," Maddie replied.

Charlotte laughed outright

"No laughing matter," said Maddie. "I did, had a little fling, couple of years ago when I first arrived. Nothing came of it, moved on now, not enough empathy he said, but it was fun at the time."

"Isn't he married?" asked Charlotte, intrigued.

"Oh yes, another Professor of Law, she's been here

once or twice, calls him Oleevay, he calls her Cherry - but her name's Beryl Pollard, a short squat black-bunned woman with thick round glasses and a big bit of a moustache. They've been married about twenty years, no children, and he's terrified of her, but that doesn't stop him!"

"And you?" queried Charlotte.

"Happily divorced. He was a Lloyd's broker and I worked with him, but I caught him covering non-insurable risks and we kicked each other out. He's still a Lloyd's broker; and I went to work for the Insurance Brokers' Registration Council in the hope of getting my own back, but I never did."

"What's that Council for?" Charlotte asked.

"Serves no useful purpose whatsoever. There's a 1977 Act under which anyone in business as an insurance broker is supposed to register and be gently regulated, but anyone who doesn't want to, any old rogue, simply calls himself 'insurance consultant' or 'insurance services' and the Act doesn't apply. I felt totally frustrated and jumped at the chance of escaping."

"And aren't you frustrated now?" Charlotte could not quite master the managerial leer.

"Bless you, no, dearie, I've become a grey groupie - I have gentlemen friends who take good care of me. Actually, at the moment, I'm going out, or more often stopping in - he's got a *pied-a-terre* in the Barbican - with another Lloyd's underwriter, Jerry Harman, over 60 but pretty vigorous and generously rich! But it won't last, he'll go back to his wife too at the first whiff of suspicion. And what about you?" Maddie demanded.

Chapter Two

"Still married, not too happily, just gone back to my maiden name - I'm Ms Angus I am and don't you forget it! But isn't there some work to be done?" This was a diversionary tactic which worked, for a while.

"That's your extra-specially selected pile of cases," gestured Maddie.

Charlotte saw a dozen or so files of various thicknesses stacked tidily at the distant end of the long oblong table which dominated the room and in front of which she had been interviewed. Where Maddie sat there were more files, plus loose papers, not stacked tidily. The room itself was rectangular with windows all along one side; blown-up photo portraits of Lady Cocks and of BIG's Bob graced each end wall whilst framed posters illustrating BIG's various publicity campaigns lined the side wall. No trace of any Ombudsman, no books, no filing cabinets, but a side-table with the coffee-machine and there were ten chairs.

"What happens when Council meets?" asked Charlotte.

"God knows, they don't come here - Marian books a private-dining room at the Hotel Russell down the road. That way they can avoid risking contamination from us and concentrate on what really interests them - eating, drinking and talking important. The Prof gets summoned to attend bits of the meetings and is then sent away to give us 'feed-back' - but it always comes across as sound-off!"

"So we never see Council members?"

"We should be so lucky," snorted Maddie. "Cocksey pops in once a week, spends half-an-hour or so in with

Marian, then parades around the office condescending before disappearing with her shopping. And there's drinks in here with the full cast at Christmas - spreading bad will all about."

"But we do have a lot of dealings with the two BIG reps on Council," she continued.

"You mean Arms and Fingers?" asked Charlotte.

"Oh, the Prof's been talking. Yes they handle the complaints from BIG's end - the idea is to get them to settle if you think there's anything in the complaint - easier with Arms, he's susceptible to my charms - but mostly there isn't. See what my Ma made for me."

Maddie pointed to three peculiar pottery creations on the window-sill. Charlotte thought she saw a flattened bird, a fat frog and a deformed mammal.

Maddie explained: "A dead duck, a lying toad and hypocritical hippo - representative of most punters, at least according to BIG's boys."

"But the Ombudsman told me he upheld a third of the complaints?" queried Charlotte.

"True - 1 in 3 sounds not so bad. If we can't get a settlement out of BIG, despite massaging Arms or Fingers - egos, not bodies - we draft a 'decision letter' for the Prof to sign."

"And does he?"

"Not necessarily," said Maddie, "nor does he always agree with letters turning punters down. And even if he agrees with the decision, he might not like your literary style - you'll have to learn to parody his. Need to lard your text with dozens of so-called equitable maxims - 'substance not form', 'look on that as done

CHAPTER TWO

which ought to be done', and 'equity acts on the conscience.' He uses a red BIC to scribble on drafts - only old Hard-on can decipher his writing - and sometimes he forgets where he is and awards marks. Failures are not unknown! Or we'll be called in for a tutorial, especially if he thinks he's spotted a 'point of law'. You'll obviously be his ideal student - and these are your first assignments, all hand-picked by me but vetted by himself as it happens."

As Charlotte put her coffee cup down and reached curiously for the top file, the door opened and the Ombudsman announced:

"First day, welcoming drinks must be a good idea!"

It was already noon.

"Stefano's?" enquired Maddie.

"Of course, you collect the terrible twins and I'll escort Charlotte along.

Oh dear, she thought, but he made no passes.

The Ombudsman and his enhanced bevy of beauties, coated against the cold, straggled towards Holborn Tube station. A self-effacing doorway led steeply down, not to trains, but to a spacious basement wine bar and restaurant, all empty. They took two tables together in the bar area, dimly lit, dumped coats on chairs. Then Ollie the jolly, host with the most, ordered:

"One red, one white to be going on with, and a bottle of fizzy water, if you please. Bill for me."

"Oui oui, monsieur G!"

"She's Spanish," said Maddie, "the rest pretend to be Italian."

Charlotte looked around. Both waitresses had long

legs and short skirts, wide smiles and foreign accents.

"Maybe that's why we come here so often," whispered Maddie, "but the barman's not bad either."

He was an Italian film star in type.

"Old enough for you?" Charlotte asked.

"He'd age, quickly."

The bar snacks were also Italian in type. Charlotte ate penne arrabiata, drank red wine and began to thaw a little towards her new colleagues. They were swapping punter stories.

"She was ironing her party dress in her undies, her boy-friend got excited, mad passionate love ensued and a hole was burnt in the dress; BIG pleaded lack of reasonable care, but we made them pay up on their 'all risks' policy; so now she's claiming for the baby!"

"He loaded all his goods and chattels into a removal van, some thief drove it off and he lost the lot; BIG wouldn't pay up because he couldn't produce any documentary evidence of ever having bought any of the allegedly lost property and we supported BIG. Two years later, same thing, van full of furniture stolen, but this time he's got purchase receipts for every single item. Arms smells a rat and so do I!"

"Talking of rats, mice nibbled the carpets, no damage cover, so he claimed for theft."

"Puppies destroyed my chap's sofa - he read the policy and pointed to 'collision with the home. . . by animals' - that contemplates rhinos!"

"Storm damage to fences was, as always, excluded but his wasn't a fence, it was 'a wooden perimeter wall'"

"Burglar stole the burglar alarm!"

Chapter Two

"The policy plainly covered damage caused by escape of water from any domestic installation, so why wouldn't BIG pay to have her clothes cleaned? Her incontinence bag had leaked!"

Ho! Ho! Ho! thought Charlotte, the duck, the toad and the hippo, all present and incorrect.

Chapter Three

Workadays

Mid-afternoon, still her first day, not better for the alcoholic outing but feeling welcomed, Charlotte began a superficial survey of her specially selected caseload. She was not to know that one of the cases constituted a hospital pass: a file with a problem, re-allocated without malice, but a poisoned chalice capable of hospitalising her, the Ombudsman, the scheme and BIG itself. Could it have been foreseen as too dangerous and cautiously dropped?

Unwarned and unalarmed, Charlotte finished an initial, superficial survey of the files. Fortunately none of the cases seemed urgent enough to insist upon immediate attention, much less action. After all they had been left to await her arrival and should surely also await a recovery of her capacity for concentration. So, overloaded with detail and undermined by drink, she ended the day, her brain hurting. Having closed and piled the files on the table, she put on her coat and scarf. Maddie's head was deep down in a dismantled bundle of correspondence. Charlotte attracted her attention by saying:

"I'll feel better tomorrow."

"Oh, sure you will - so will we all, with any luck. See you a lot Lottie!" Maddie, appearing to be perfectly in possession of herself if not her faculties, was obviously accustomed to consuming virtually liquid lunches without displaying undue disorientation.

Must be practice, thought Charlotte, perhaps the Ombudsman will coach me too.

She struggled home - Holborn Tube again, then Liverpool Street to Chelmsford, on foot through the cold and dark to their deceptively spacious family semi, half way down a cul de sac with long back gardens opening onto the gloom of Admiral's Park. Easy access in either direction, she thought again, but they had yet to be burgled and the twins had still to escape for long enough to worry the police. Thus she made her first return from ombudsmanic affairs to domestic disharmony.

In the following days and weeks, she worked her way through the special selection of case-files, not enthusiastically at the outset but with increasing energy and interest. Thirteen files, one booby-trapped but not the file at the top of the pile.

First file - the Jewellery Case

Charlotte found the story stimulating. David and Sophie Neuberger chose to celebrate their silver wedding with a second honeymoon: not Southend this time but a week in the Loire at a Chateau-Hotel, half-board, living in luxury like French aristocrats. Driving from Hackney, overnight crossing from Portsmouth to Cherbourg, just out of season in September, 1988. Determined to dress as a duchess, Sophie took all her jewellery - nearly £45,000 worth, she claimed, of necklaces and rings given to her by David over the years, apart from her engagement, wedding and eternity rings which she always wore.

Before embarking, arriving early, they left their Ford Sierra in a public car park near the harbour, went for a short walk and relished their last supper of British 'take-away' fish and chips, at least for a while. Fearing mugging, Sophie locked her jewellery in the glove compartment rather than wearing it. Eating as they walked, they returned to disaster: quarter-lights smashed, luggage ransacked, oddments missing, radio stolen, could be worse but - glove-compartment open and empty! Police called, ferry missed.

David's motor insurance paid for the window and the radio. His travel insurance paid for the unwanted night's stay in Portsmouth and delayed crossing. Neither would pay for Sofie's jewellery - value limits exceeded. However the jewellery was specifically covered by David's household policy, even outside the house. This, as luck would have it, was a BIG policy. But BIG declined payment, the letter of 'declinature' - insurers' jargon for rejection - pointed to a 'lack of reasonable care' exclusion.

It had been Chip's case so Charlotte asked her about it.

"Insurers never pay-up for jewellery - or watches or money - on principle. Couldn't have been stolen if reasonable care had been taken - policyholders have a common law duty to take care of their valuables, they say, even if this isn't spelled out in the small print. No care, no pay. Should be kept locked in a safe. Stupid

CHAPTER THREE

really, jewellery has to be worn sometimes, but here I actually sympathised with BIG. Worth far too much to be left in the car," said Chip. "However, the Prof wasn't sure, thought there was a legal point, so you'd better ask him."

Charlotte poked her head round his open door and wondered, hesitantly, if she could have a word.

"Of course, any time," said he enthusiastically, covering up the book he had been studying - but not before Charlotte had read its title: *Better Bridge Bidding*. Reading documents, especially letters, upside down on partners' desks is one of the most valuable practical skills acquired by solicitors during their training as articled clerks.

"This jewellery case, Neuberger, lack of reasonable care, Chip says there might be a point of law."

"Well, basically BIG - that's Arms really - doesn't think people should take jewellery on holiday with them at all. If they do, should be at their own risk. But their policies don't say that and two or three years ago there was a High Court decision against Phoenix Assurance where jewellery had been pinched from a baggage trolley at an airport - judge said the reasonable care condition 'mustn't become a trap for the unwary', only gross or blatant negligence would justify rejection of claims. Arms hasn't come to terms with this yet - look the case up and have a word with him. Tell him we can't decide against punters when the courts would be for them, whatever we think of the merits, otherwise this scheme is pointless."

So she did have a word with Arms, on the phone.

"Who? Oh you're Ollie's new girl, the brilliant lawyer! We must have a drink sometime, I'll get in touch next time in town, eh? Now this Neuberger chancer, Ollie's bound to favour him - Jews always scratch each other's backs - but my nose tells me this is dodgy one: that jewellery's still under the floorboards in Hackney, mark my words, he's paying for the holiday by this claim, he hopes, and holidays for the rest of his life. Over my dead body! The industry's plagued with this sort of fraud, sooner or later we've got to make a stand, for the sake of honest policyholders. And the Prudential is doing exactly that. You'd do best to wait for the decision in their case before making your mind up on this one. Never forget, if you go too far, we'll have to seriously consider whether the scheme's worth while - we'll be paying claims that our competitors don't have to and that's not a level playing field."

"Arms is always threatening like that, but the scheme is big Bob's baby, whether he likes it or not," said the Prof. "However, this time I think he's right, you should wait and see what happens in the courts."

So she did. The Prudential lost comprehensively in the High Court and the Court of Appeal[1]: the test was whether the policyholder had acted recklessly and if precautionary steps had been taken, even ineffective ones - like hiding jewellery in a locked glove compartment, the insurer would fail to prove lack of reasonable care. Attributing the decision to undue influence on the part of the judges' wives but accepting the inevitable, BIG paid-up in full. Arms was unhappy.

1. Reported eventually as and at *Sofi v Prudential Assurance Co.* [1993] Lloyd's Law Report 559 CA.

CHAPTER THREE

A private detective was hired to check out David Neuberger's, and Sofie's, dealings with jewellery. To no avail, so far.

"As it happens," mused the Ombudsman one evening at Stefano's, "I might have met the Neubergers. We were in the Loire region at the time. Wife's a Francophile, always have to holiday in France."

"In September?" queried Charlotte, drinking Italian red.

Ollie drank too. "Yes, not high season, not so hot, no school children, not *vacances* for the French but still vacation for the university - and cheaper. We didn't stay in a chateau like aristocrats but in a *gîte* like *vrai* peasants. But we visited chateaux - averaged two a day for a fortnight - came back chateaued and shattered."

Ignoring his little witticism, as well worth ignoring, and thinking his French pronunciation excruciatingly English, Charlotte said, "So you tasted a lot at every visit."

"Not those sort of chateaux, all stately homes or quasi-museums, and any way I was doing the driving - Beryl navigates."

"No drinking at all!"

"I didn't say that - our *gîte* was actually an apartment in *Rochfort-sur-Loire*, home of *Domaines des Baumard*: producers of a sparkling earthy rosé called *Carte Corail*, also the sublime *Clos du Papillon* from *Savennières* and their opulent *Quarts de Chaume*, sweet you know."

He's waxing lyrical, thought Charlotte, wish he'd wane.

"And a muralled tasting hall, certainly justifying

43

more than one visit."

Per day? Charlotte wondered.

"But I don't recall the Neubergers: 'Oh fat white woman whom David finds thrilly, Why do you walk through the salons without any jewellery?'" He chuckled happily to himself.

Yuk! she thought, but simply said: "Sofie's brown and skinny," and asked: "Are you Jewish?"

"On the contrary, I was brought up a good atheist!"

Charlotte drank up. Chelmsford called: the twins to bed, spouse to be fed; unless, hopefully, Rosa had again attended to their needs. Then aerobics, perhaps, at the Institute, keep fit classes really, before reading herself asleep. A drink with Ollie en route, conveniently coincidental at first, was quickly becoming a custom.

"Till to-morrow," said he.

She set off thinking of holidays, with last August in Jersey indigestibly in mind: slimy Simon supposed spouse and father yachting, herself and the twins, Dan and Ben, abandoned in an old folks' home masquerading as a hotel - the residents, initially 'ah'ing' over her beautiful boys, had rapidly tired of their noise and naughtiness, as she had herself. Slimy and the flower-pot things!

Chapter four

Witness Day

Arriving earlyish a few days later, Charlotte climbed the stairs and, to her slight astonishment, found the office door open and sexy Sarah not only there but also in a state of exceptional excitement. Standing stolidly at reception, scrutinising her closely as a new arrival, was a dourly bored youth, drably dressed in a voluminous grey overcoat with his hands deep in the side pockets. His appearance seemed ominously familiar.

"Lottie, thank goodness you're early - I didn't know what to do and Mr Wood's away today learning about computers. Was it right to let him in? He's not a policyholder but from some lawyers and now he's waiting for Professor Goodman," said Sarah. "Wants to serve him with something official!"

Of course, recognised Charlotte, her life as a litigation practitioner flooding back, she knew the type: an outdoor clerk - a sort of specialist 'gofer' employed by firms of solicitors having frequent need to lodge documents and make applications at the Royal Courts of Justice in the Strand. He would also be used to serve notices of appeal, copies of affidavits, by-hand 'without prejudice' letters and all such course of action papers on other parties to judicial proceedings.

"It's alright," she said to Sarah, turning to the youth: "You don't have to wait - as his solicitor I can accept service

LOVE AT ALL RISKS

on his behalf. My authority extends to receiving any court matters." Well, impliedly perhaps, and my curiosity certainly extends that far, she only told herself.

"Nah," shrugged the dour youth. "Gotta be in person. Summons for 'sarternoon."

"Please yourself - but it could be a long wait, Professor Goodman's time-keeping is not as regular as clockwork, especially in the morning. Meanwhile I'll make some coffee. Like a cup?"

"OK fanks - if it's no bovver."

"Sit down - you won't be able to miss him, no other men here, but if there's any risk of him sneaking in past you, Miss Potts can be relied on to draw you to his attention."

Charlotte went off down the corridor to the Council Chamber. No sign of Maddie yet. So she took the coffee pot and cups on a tray back past reception, smiling sweetly at Sarah and the youth, to wash them all and fill the pot with water in the 'rest room'. Returning she observed that Sarah had started to cheer the dour youth up.

"Shouldn't be too long now," Charlotte told the youth, "the coffee, that is. Incidentally, I really am the solicitor, you know."

The filter-coffee machine had begun to splutter and fill the pot when Maddie walked in.

"Christ, you're early, Lottie! Did you stop in town? And, if so, where and who'd you sleep with? Speaking of which, who's Sarah brought to work on?"

"He's got a summons to serve on the Prof," Charlotte replied to the last question, rightly regarding the rest as rhetorical. "Wouldn't give it to me but Sarah may do

CHAPTER FOUR

better."

"She was hanging his coat up when I came in - saw huge inside pockets stuffed with papers," said Maddie.

"The mark of the outdoor clerk!"

No explanation was offered or sought, other aspects of the situation attracting greater interest.

"Do you think she'll get any more off him?" Maddie continued.

"Clothes or information?" asked Charlotte, pouring coffee for four.

Taking two cups towards reception, Charlotte was just in time to see Ollie arrive and be served. Sarah jumped up from a seat beside the no longer dour youth.

"Ooh! Ernie, that's him," said she, seemingly having exchanged names and allegiances.

The youth, reverting to dour, addressed Ollie sombrely: "Professor Goodman?"

"Who wants to know?" replied Ollie warily. "I make no admissions."

The youth ignored this prevarication and proceeded:

"I 'ave to serve this document on you, sir, from the 'igh court of justice."

Then he felt his jacket pockets and looked around in, it appeared, momentary panic. After this he darted over to where Sarah had hung his overcoat and pulled a long blue envelope out of one of the inside pockets. He thrust it at Ollie who raised his hands above his head, saying:

"Don't shoot - or even serve!"

"It's a witness summons plus attendance expenses in the matter of *Thomas Saunders versus The BIG Insurance Company Limited*. Court 26 'sarternoon from 2 o'clock.

Take it or I'll drop it right 'ere on the floor - it'll count as good service!"

"Oh is that all," said Ollie taking the envelope and looking relieved. "I've been looking forward to this!"

The Ombudsman hurried off to his corner room without another word to anyone. Charlotte's curiosity was becoming acute but she knew better than to quiz the clerk - no one would have bothered to tell him what it was actually all about. So she simply put down the cups of coffee on the reception desk, saying:

"Not such a long wait after all - and no trouble from him! Have some coffee anyway and finish your chat up."

Did the dour youth blush a bit?

"Fanks, but you ain't really a solicitor eh?"

"Ask Sarah, she knows about soliciting." Maddie had come out of the Council Chamber only to hear the last question. "What's happening?"

Charlotte rolled her eyes up at Sarah and the youth, told them to take no notice of her articled clerk.

Back in the Council Chamber she asked Maddie whether she had heard of the *Thomas Saunders* affair.

"Oh yes, caused us a stir last year - the Prof was fucking furious!"

"Mind your French, you blighter, and tell me about it."

Apparently, a prospering young executive, called Tom Saunders, newly married, had purchased the matrimonial home, a town house in Esher, with the aid of an endowment mortgage. This financial package had been sold as an integral whole by one of BIG's appointed representatives, a Mr Hart, although the mortgage was with the Masham Building Society. During his marketing pitch, the rep had,

Chapter Four

allegedly, made promises about the level and variability of the interest rate on the mortgage loan and failed to disclose penal redemption charges. Tom had brought a complaint to the Ombudsman that those promises had been broken, with the unacceptable consequence that the proceeds of the linked endowment policy might not be enough to pay off the loan and interest on maturity in 15 years time. He wanted to change to a repayment mortgage and cancel the policy. Neither BIG nor the Building Society would agree, particularly because Mr Hart was reluctant to relinquish his commission: BIG would have allowed Tom to surrender the policy, but the surrender value was nil for the first 5 years and anyway the Masham objected. Since mortgages were not subject to any effective consumer complaints arrangements, Tom had come to Ollie. A complainant right up the street of a former professor of conveyancing!

However, BIG objected strenuously to this complaint being investigated by their Ombudsman. The objections came from BIG generally, not just from Fingers the finance director who had created the endowment mortgage scheme but also from big Bob the Managing Director who had created the Insurance Ombudsman Scheme. Outside jurisdiction they had said. But Ollie had relied on his published Terms of Reference, which conferred power to receive "*complaints, disputes and claims made in connection with or arising out of policies of insurance*". His understandably simplistic opinion was that, like a horse and carriage, the endowment and the mortgage went together: a complaint about one part must be connected with the other part. So he had proposed proceeding.

However once again, the Ombudsman had reckoned without Council. BIG's Bob had fixed a deal with Lady Cocks, and therefore with the rest of Council, whereby this question of jurisdiction should be referred to arbitration. The chosen arbitrator was the media known barrister, Hugo Bolsover QC. "Balls-off and balls-up," the Prof had been heard to say, often apparently. This learned silk adopted what he called a "purposive" construction of the Terms of Reference. This led him to conclude that the Scheme was "insurance specific" so that a complaint about a mortgage, albeit a mortgage connected with a policy of insurance, lacked sufficient nexus. The outcome of this clever reasoning, naturally lacking any nexus with the real world, was that Ollie could not proceed with Tom Saunders' complaint.

The essential elements of the Thomas Saunders affair had not taken Maddie long to explain and, as she finished the story so far, the door to their room slammed open. There stood the Ombudsman, mug in one hand and blue envelope in the other, grinning like a maniac, thought Charlotte apprehensively.

"Litigator Lottie - I need you on escort duty!" he cried. "To take me to your courts!"

Fearing the effects of childish over-excitement on a middle-aged Ombudsman, Charlotte took his mug to pour him coffee, saying:

"Sit down and tell us what's happening, slowly and quietly."

He handed her the envelope and sat down.

"You'll find two £5 notes - not a bribe, travelling expenses - we could take a taxi, but it's walking distance,

CHAPTER FOUR

better to spend it on celebratory drinks after!"

"After what?" Charlotte tried to insist.

"There's also the witness summons in the envelope - present myself at Court 26 at 2 pm today or be held in contempt - ah ha - nothing would keep me away!"

"But exactly why do you have to be there?"

"Well last year a punter called Tom Saunders complained to us about his endowment mortgage..." Ollie began seriously.

"Yes yes," Charlotte hastily interrupted, not yet wanting another lecture. "I know the story so far - arbitration, no jurisdiction, complaint rejected. Just tell me the latest instalment."

"I was cross about that," said Ollie. "Endowment mortgages are over-sold by greedy insurance reps - not only BIG's boys - and they're not going to meet homeowners' expectations. Repayment mortgages would be right for most punters, but no commission for the rep. There'll be a public scandal soon, mark my words."

"Go on Prof, go on for God's sake," Maddie now urged him back to the story.

"Good old Tom - young executive Tom actually - he didn't take rejection of his complaint lying down, instructed solicitors and started legal proceedings against BIG for breach of promise by their rep. I was delighted when I learnt of this, because the bloody arbitration had been kept private - no adverse publicity."

Nor favourable publicity for the consumer's champion, thought Charlotte, but she merely asked:

"How does this involve you, though?"

"Tom's solicitors wrote asking me to give evidence on

his behalf, but it didn't seem to me appropriate for an Ombudsman to be seen to take sides in litigation, especially since Council opposed the idea."

"Cocksie threatened to sack him!" Maddie screached.

"Not exactly," said Ollie. "Lady Cocks simply communicated to me the fact that, if I voluntarily became a witness against BIG in court, she was confident that Council would find it difficult to recommend renewal of my appointment. She also said that big Bob might wind the Scheme up straightaway in the face of bad publicity."

"I see," said Charlotte. "You think it'll be different if you're forced to go by a summons."

"Of course, there'll be no option and I'll be treated as a hostile witness!"

Hostile to whom, she wondered, smelling a put-up job. Surely he'd have had more notice than on the day? Had he inadvertently, or even deliberately, pressed a self-destruct button?

So at one o'clock precisely the Ombudsman and his Assistant Solicitor set off for the Law Courts. Ollie carried a black briefcase containing his *Saunders v BIG* file and wore a smile as well as a short raincoat over that green corduroy suit. Charlotte carried a brown briefcase containing a notebook and wore a frown as well as her winter coat over, as it happened, a green trouser suit. Witnesses maybe, she was thinking, but not female solicitors in green suits - he should have warned me.

"Cheer up," he said. "I'll stick to the facts and leave opinions for others."

"Humph," she said.

They walked down Kingsway, turning off left before

CHAPTER FOUR

Aldwych so as to pass behind the London School of Economics and enter the Courts by the back Carey Street entrance. This had been Charlotte's chosen route.

"To avoid the Press at the Strand entrance. . ."

Ollie had looked a touch disappointed, so she smirked, adding:

". . . and it's very much quicker."

The walk took them only a quarter of an hour and she led him downstairs from the back entrance to the Courts' cafeteria.

"We're in plenty of time - if I remember rightly Court 26 is virtually next door. I'll go and check and see what's listed and who's sitting while you lurk in here, inconspicuously if possible!"

Ollie did not protest at these instructions but simply said:

"Okey dokey, I'll join the queue and spend some of our expenses on coffee and sandwiches."

"Hope they're edible nowadays. Back soon."

They sat cramped together chewing ham and cheese rolls amidst other depressed and bewildered customers of the Courts and of its cafeteria. The *cappuccino*, machine made, was English style - much like a bedtime drink.

"Nobody there now, of course, but *Saunders v BIG* is the only case on the list. Being heard by Mr Justice Palmer. Newly elevated when I was practising. Macho judge - showing-off how quickly he could get rid of the business. Read the papers, came into Court with his mind made up, not only wouldn't listen to anything else but would argue against it himself. Difficult for counsel on the wrong end to deal with - known as a 'lottery judge'" Charlotte was not necessarily encouraging Ollie, but he only observed:

"He was in my year at College, known as 'palmy Palmer', as in cross mine with silver. Always intended going to the Bar. Didn't like me - his exam results were never as good!"

At ten to two they left the cafeteria, as did everyone else. Outside Court 26 Ollie was greeted warmly by a squat bald scruffy-suited solicitor-type.

"Prof Goodman! Glad to see you made it here. Do you know the client, Mr Saunders?"

"Hello, Ron," said the Ombudsman, shaking his hand and that of the already balding young executive with him. "And Mr Saunders, whom I feel I know well, though we've not actually met."

"And this is Chrissie Marshall, our barrister," continued Ron genially, indicating a neatly miserable bespectacled young woman covered in black robes and looking distinctly uncomfortable in a very white wig.

"Lottie, meet Ron Silk, Tom's solicitor," said Ollie, "and Ron, meet Charlotte Angus, my solicitor."

"Just a minute, just a minute - aren't you supposed to be an unwilling witness?" The introductions were interrupted by Charlotte. "We'd better separate before the other side get the right idea!"

She could see a group, including Fingers, around a large fat uncouthly bearded dirty-wigged barrister, all regarding them closely and curiously. They were standing further down the cavernous corridor near the other door to Court 26.

"Ah! Afternoon, Mr Lightman - you've met my lawyer, Ms Angus?" Ollie had moved over to the opposing group,

Chapter Four

Charlotte hurrying with him. Fingers did not seem pleased to see them.

"You're not supposed to be here - the MD won't like it."

"No option, old chap, witness summons - look - prison for me on failure to attend!"

Fingers' face suggested that he thought prison a not inappropriate place for BIG's Ombudsman.

"Come on now, we'd better go in before it's too late," said Charlotte, the minder, retrieving Ollie, the mindless of danger.

They pushed through the half of the swing doors that could swing and went into the courtroom.

"Back row with the spectators, I think, and await the call, quietly." Charlotte spoke firmly, as if to the twins but hoping some notice would be taken. There were, however, no spectators.

The BIG group crowded into the front row to their right, except for the fat barrister who barged up and down in the second row, the privileged preserve along with book rests of leading counsel. In contrast, to their left little Miss Marshall crept into the third row, as if to steerage space to which junior counsel were confined, without book rests and discriminatorily distanced from the driver or judge, at least so Charlotte had always thought. Behind Miss Marshall sat Saunders and Silk. Clerks and ushers wandered purposefully around like disgruntled schoolteachers ready to control unruly pupils.

"Court rise!"

All present stood. Stage left, as it were, entered a stately robed gentleman wearing half-moon glasses who bowed towards them showing the top of his head with white straggly hair around a spreading bald spot. He looked aged to Charlotte. But then he slapped a hand to his head and hastily left the way he had entered only to reappear a moment later, this time be-wigged and merely nodding. He now looked younger to Charlotte. After this performance, Mr Justice Palmer sat down and so did all present except Miss Marshall.

"Yes Miss uhm Marshall?"

"If it please your lordship, I now call my last witness, Professor Goodman." Her voice was obviously raised so as to be heard and so sounded unnaturally shrill. She continued speaking quickly. "Perhaps I should explain straightaway that Professor Goodman was reluctant to give any evidence at all in this case and is attending only because of a summons so to do."

Whilst she spoke, Ollie rose and processed professorially towards the witness box, gazing ahead into the distance with all the *gravitas* traditionally displayed at university ceremonials. Arriving at the box, he stepped up, turned to the nearest clerk and announced in clarion tones:

"Having been brought up a devout atheist, it is my wish to affirm!"

The judge, however, was ignoring him and said:

"Yes, Mr Bolsover?"

The big fat barrister towered in front of little Miss Marshall, who sat unhappily down.

"With me learned friend's permission, M'Lud, I rise in support of Professor Goodman's reluctance to appear as a witness in this case. As your lordship may appreciate, the

CHAPTER FOUR

good Professor is the so-called 'ombudsman' under a claims handling scheme sponsored and, indeed, funded by my client. Since it is of the essence that he is supposed to consider policyholders' claims independently and impartially, it would, I submit, be entirely inappropriate for the Professor to become embroiled in any consequential litigation suggesting partisanship."

"The expedient course, in my judgment, is for me to interrogate Professor Goodman briefly as to his eligibility as a witness before wasting any further time."

"Yes, M'Lud," said Bolsover, slumping back down.

"You agree, Miss Marshall?"

"If it please your lordship."

Ollie was not consulted, Charlotte observed without surprise and prepared herself to take a note of the interrogations.

Judge: "Now Mr Goodman, you are, so I am given to understand, the insurance 'ombudsman'. What exactly does that mean?"

Ombudsman: "As most educated adults will certainly know, it's a word of Scandinavian origin signifying 'grievance man' or people's representative against the establishment..."

Judge: "Yes, yes - I do, of course, recall the enactment of the Parliamentary Commissioner Act - in 1967 was it not - our English 'ombudsman'. From what statute do you purport to derive authority?"

Ombudsman: "No statute - it's a voluntary scheme established by the BIG Insurance Company."

Judge (sounding like Lady Bracknell about a handbag):

"Voluntary?"

Ombudsman: "Absolutely - BIG has arranged that any of their policyholders who's had a claim rejected can have it adjudicated by me."

Judge: "Ah, I see now - this is arbitration by another name, but smelling just the same, eh?"

Ombudsman: "Absolutely not! There are at least three significant distinctions. Firstly, there's no clause in the policy obliging the policyholder to submit his claim to me. He can take it straight off to court if he wants to - and can afford to. Secondly, he won't be bound by my decision, he can still go off to court, but BIG will be bound. . ."

Judge: "On what basis can BIG possibly be bound? Can't be in contract, since there's no provision in the policy. And any agreement directly with you for the benefit of claimants would surely be difficult for them to sue on. But never mind, what's your third distinction? Incidentally, you could address me properly as 'my lord'."

Ombudsman: "I suppose I could. However, the third point is that my decisions can turn simply upon what I consider fair and reasonable in all the circumstances, not necessarily according to the law."

Judge (Lady Bracknell again): "Not according to *law*?"

Ombudsman: "The point's hardly novel! If your worship were able to cast his mind back to Keeton's lectures on 'Equity and Trusts', you might perhaps remember that in 1875 the Court of Chancery finally prevailed over the Common Law Courts. . ."

Judge: "Of course I remember, only too well - instead of certainty, equity varied with the length of the Chancellor's foot. Now no doubt it'll depend on the length of an

CHAPTER FOUR

Ombudsman's nose - short shrift with you, eh? Ha, ha!"

Fat barrister Bolsover laughed immoderately at this judicial witticism, whilst Miss Marshall, along with Charlotte, only chuckled a little and politely. But Ollie also grinned a bit: his nose was indubitably snub.

Judge again: "But seriously, a decision reached otherwise than in accordance with the law could not conceivably be enforceable. What was it the late, great Lord Scrutton said? 'There can be no Arcadia where the Queen's writ does not run!'[2] I've no doubt that Her Majesty's judges would regard these 'ombudsmanic' arrangements as contrary to public policy!"[3]

Ombudsman persisting: "But the BIG Insurance Company has announced that it will comply with my awards up to £100,000..."

Judge interrupting: "That's completely different - if BIG chooses to honour your non-legal decisions by making *ex gratia* payments, it is, of course free so to do. Enforcement is another question altogether."

---

2. What Lord Justice Scrutton actually said was: "In my view to allow English citizens to agree to exclude this safeguard from the administration of the law [ie appeal to the courts on questions of law] is contrary to public policy. There must be no Alsatia in England where the King's writ does not run. It seems quite clear that no British Court would recognise or enforce an agreement of British citizens not to raise a defence of illegality by British Law." See *Czernikow v Roth, Schmidt and Co.* [1922] 2 KB 478 at p.488. Cp. now s.46(1)(b) of the Arbitration Act 1996 belatedly allowing 'equity clauses' in arbitration.

3. However compare Lord Justice Rose in *R v Insurance Ombudsman ex parte Aegon Life Assurance Ltd* [1995] Lloyd's Reinsurance Law Reports 101 at pp.105-6: ". . . the public do not have to use the Ombudsman. They can sue insurers in the courts. If they go before the Ombudsman, because he is not limited to purely legal considerations, in many cases their prospects of success will be better. But they have the choice of forum. Likewise, for insurers, although there are the advantages of Bureau membership to which I have referred, membership is not obligatory. Those who choose to be members run a greater risk of an adverse decision of complaint is made to the Ombudsman than if the case were decided in the courts by reference to strictly legal principles."

Ombudsman stubbornly: "And also, unlike an arbitrator, my procedures are inquisitorial, not adversarial. Instead of reaching a decision after listening to debating points like you do, I proactively investigate the merits with a view to discovering all the facts and genuinely doing justice!"

Judge querulously: "Do your proactive investigations afford the defendant insurer the same substantive and procedural safeguards of a trial in court? Are there documentary pleadings so that the case to be answered can be known? Surely BIG is not so bad that it needs to suffer your sort of procedures!"

Ombudsman angrily: "The Ombudsman movement is growing, not because insurers and others investigated are particularly bad, but because of extreme dissatisfaction with the courts - slow, costly, legalistic and overwhelmed with formalities. After all one man's safeguard is another man's hurdle! BIG's commendable idea was to level the playing-field and let their policyholders have access to free, fair and informal decisions without the fancy dress!"

Judge blanching: "Well, be all that as it may, let us turn away from these no doubt fascinating, albeit academic, issues of alternative dispute resolution and consider instead your precise rôle in this case in front of me. Am I to understand that you actually investigated Mr Saunders' claim?"

Ombudsman hesitantly: "Strictly, no I didn't, but. . ."

Judge interrupting again: "Why not?"

Ombudsman unhappily: "It was deemed that his

Chapter Four

complaint fell outside my jurisdiction."

Judge happily: "Thank you Mr Goodman. That will be enough. Articulate as always - I well recall your, ah, forthright interventions in seminars at the outset of our respective careers - you have made your position very clear. Consequently I have been able to come to the conclusion that you are entirely right - you are in no sense a competent witness, much less a compellable one. Your 'ombudsman' appointment on behalf of the BIG Insurance Company is essentially as an 'in-house' claims handler. Final stage, I accept, by gratuitous agreement, but lacking any judicial or even quasi-judicial status. In any event, for present purposes, you can have nothing admissible, or worthwhile, to contribute since you did not actually embark upon any investigation of the plaintiff's allegations. There has been no suggestion that you could otherwise have acquired relevant knowledge of material facts. Accordingly I am glad to rule, as you evidently wished, that the Court need not detain you further from your endeavours to obtain justice, as you see it, for the defendant's policyholders. You may step down."

Seeming somewhat stunned, certainly into silence, Ollie rejoined Charlotte at the back of the courtroom. The stately *gravitas* of the professorial procession to the witness box was absent, she felt, his movements having become rather more reminiscent of scuttling schoolboys. He looked at her with vastly raised eyebrows, then winked and whispered:

"At least there was nothing for Fingers to complain

about. So my giving evidence shouldn't scupper the scheme after all!"

But has his spat from student days scuppered Tom Saunders, she wondered. Nevertheless, she reflected, his spirited restatement of the ombudsman credo in teeth of a hostile judge carried conviction - a valiant if futile attempt, not unlike the Charge of the Light Brigade.

"Ah, yes of course, Miss Marshall. Do you have anything to add to your submissions of this morning?" His Honour, Mr Justice Palmer, proposed proceeding with the case.

"No milord." A miserable meek reply following a short shake of the head from solicitor Silk.

The fat barrister lurched to his feet to receive a humourless judicial smile.

"I don't need to trouble you further Mr Bolsover. The claim can be safely dismissed in the light of what is already in front of me."

"Very good, M'Lud."

The fat barrister subsided, evidently surprised but not deflated.

His lordship rehearsed the arguments for and the evidence given by the plaintiff Saunders, whom he found an unsatisfactory witness. Not compared to Ollie, thought Charlotte. Mr Bolsover's destructive cross-examination of the plaintiff was commended whilst Missie Marshall's submissions were restated and rubbished.

"Accordingly, I am wholly unable to find, even on the balance of probabilities, that the alleged

CHAPTER FOUR

representations were in fact made, never mind understood to be, or relied upon as, a promise relating to the level of the mortgage interest rates from time to time. This suffices to dispose of the action on the facts. However, in appreciation of where I am sitting, I should for completeness add a word or two on the law."

"Perhaps the pompous palmy will go too far," whispered Ollie. That'll make a matching pair, thought Charlotte.

"In my judgment," Mr Justice Palmer continued, "there is no equitable jurisdiction to hold a person to a promise simply because the court thought it unfair, unconscionable or morally objectionable for him to go back on it. If there were such jurisdiction one might as well forget the law of contract and judge every civil dispute with a portable palm tree. The days of justice varying with the length of the Lord Chancellor's foot would have returned.[4] Even if the alleged representations had been made and the plaintiff had understood them to involve promises which he had reasonably expected to be performed, it remains quite clear that a reasonable expectation does not become a contractual right.[5] So the action must fail - presumably you are unable to resist the normal costs order, Miss Marshall?"

"No milord."

"Much obliged M'Lud."

---

[4]. For these very words, see *per* Judge Weeks QC in *Taylor v Dickens* 1997 Times Law Report 24 November.

[5]. And for this proposition, see *per* Sir Richard Scott, Vice-Chancellor, in *Equitable Life Assurance Society v Hyman* [1999] Pensions Law Reports 297 at para.97.

"Court rise!"

Outside in the corridor Charlotte began to realise that things were not necessarily as they seemed. To start with, she had seen Miss Marshall, instead of dissolving in tears as anticipated, engaged in a sparkling conversation with Bolsover the bounder, just as if they had both won. After that she saw Tom Saunders shake hands with a flashily dressed chunky chap she took to be BIG's naughty rep whilst solicitor Silk shared a joke with his opposite number. Then, to cap it all, she overheard Fingers, all oily smiles, greeting Ollie and saying:

"Well done Professor! You certainly made sure that the judge didn't want to listen to you any more!"

Ollie did not look gratified - Charlotte knew that had not been his real idea - and asked:

"Have I missed a trick - what are you up to?"

"No trick exactly, but an appropriate accommodation has been reached." Fingers should be winking, thought Charlotte. "In confidence, mind, I can tell you that the Masham Building bods have agreed in writing that, if Saunders pursued his action against us and lost, they would let him change his mortgage to repayment at variable interest rates with no redemption charge. Exactly what he wants. Then, on the basis that Masham have sunk to urging a client to sue us, regretfully but justifiably we have lost confidence in our relationship with them. This, perhaps fortunately, entitles BIG to terminate the tie agreement with Masham freeing us to finalise commercially acceptable contracts elsewhere."

Chapter Four

"So it was all a put up job!"

At this Fingers did wink.

"But what about the endowment policy, that's left standing isn't it?" Charlotte had the temerity to enquire partly out of curiosity but mostly as an attempt to puncture Fingers' self-satisfaction.

"Oh no, we've done a deal with Mr Saunders - in simple terms," - he smiled patronisingly, - "he's agreed to swap it for an equivalent personal pension policy. A tax-efficient savings vehicle - and our Micky Hart keeps his commission."

"And what about the costs of this afternoon's charade? Won't be cheap - can Saunders afford to pay his own never mind yours?" Ollie remained unhappy.

"I don't think he'll find that aspect over-burdensome." Fingers nodded and winked again.

Charlotte conducted Ollie out of the Royal Courts of Justice at the back again and into Carey Street, still a euphemism for bankruptcy was the thought that occurred to her. It might have been a little too early chronologically for a drink but not spiritually. Stefano's waitresses received them as regulars and welcomed them as big spenders when Ollie ordered champagne.

"What's this in aid of, then?" Charlotte enquired suspiciously.

"Success, the future is ours! We've just achieved a publishable illustration of precisely why the courts ought to be replaced by Ombudsmen. All, I'm glad to say, courtesy of palmy Palmer. Let's drink to - wait for it - justice for the people!"

"Justice for the people - and utmost damnation to

the judiciary!"

They drank together solemnly, reviewing the day's various revelations, until eventually their usual good humour was restored and the tricks and treats of insurers and solicitors seemed of less significance.

"There's a Masham in Yorkshire, not too far from the Halifax," Ollie mused. "Didn't know it'd got a Building Society, but it has lots of little breweries. Visited Theakston's once for a guided tour and tasting - produce a really real ale, strong, thick and tasty, called 'Old Peculier' - one of my favourites, spelt with an 'e'."

Takes one to know one, thought Charlotte, spelt with an 'O'.

Chapter Five

Chequered Day

Next morning began with the customary exchange of ribald but well-meaning unpleasantries with Maddie, this time prompted by Charlotte's brief, edited account of the Ombudsman's afternoon in court, not quite Ollie's last stand. After this, coffee poured, she opened the file on another of Chip's car-connected cases. The chronologically collected correspondence disclosed, so Chip had said, an everyday story albeit one novel to Charlotte, who was realising the sheltered life she had led outside insurance.

Second file - the Case of the Unchecked Cheque

Don Dyson, in financial difficulties, had wanted to sell his car, a Renault 5, and advertised in local newspapers. One Frank Ferris turned up on Don's doorstep, test-drove the car, Don prudently sitting in the passenger seat, and pronounced himself pleased. They agreed a price. Frank wrote a cheque and handed it over. Don let him drive the car away but prudently did not hand over his log book.

"I'd better keep this until your cheque's cleared," he later said he recalled saying with a feeling of being sensible.

"Of course, no problem," he thought Frank had replied, adding: "Why can't buying a house be this easy?"

"Ha! Ha! Why not indeed?" had laughed Don, whose house would soon also be up for sale - after being repossessed by his friendly neighbourhood building society.

The cheque bounced. Don tried but failed to make contact with Frank - or his little Renault. But he was comprehensively insured and the policy covered theft. To his angry astonishment, BIG refused to pay up. Arms wrote explaining that the car had not been stolen at all: title had passed to Frank by virtue (if that is the word) of the contract for sale, so Don had only lost the proceeds of sale, money not covered by Don's motor insurance. He cited, evidently with some satisfaction, a 1955 court case against General Accident in direct support.[6]

Again Chip had agreed with BIG's Arms, although troubled by the merits. And again the Prof had disagreed:

"Surely title to the car cannot have been intended to pass until the cheque had been cleared?" he objected. "Even if Don hadn't actually said anything about clearing the cheque, this intention should be implied from retention of the log book. That 1955 decision is unfair law and I'm not going to follow it whatever Arms thinks!"

However, any immediate confrontation was avoided because, once more, Charlotte discovered, the point

---

[6]. A decision of Lord Chief Justise Goddard reported as *Eisinger v Genera Accident Fire Assurance Corporation Ltd.* [1955] 2 All England Law Reports 897 - the judgment is so short that the insured may have felt relieved to escape with his life.

was about to be retested in the courts, again against General Accident. This time the decision was different - faced with personal policyholders, today's judges dislike siding with insurers against the merits - and a line of argument not unlike the Ombudsman's prevailed.[7]

Nevertheless, Charlotte did not make BIG pay up straight-away. Not because she thought that Don had failed to take reasonable care - although Chip thought this a close call, he had hardly been reckless - but because Don had now found out where his car was: Frank had sold it on to a John Parker who lived nearby. This *bona fide* purchaser had had nothing whatsoever to do with the scam, but Charlotte reasoned the car still belonged in law to Don who had an indisputable right to recover it - strictly no loss. And she found really recent legal authority to support her.[8]

Poor John, the innocent loser, Frank having vanished, of course, with the money. But if there was to be a battle over recovery, that is as to ownership, she decided that BIG would have to fund the litigation to a successful conclusion or else meet Don's claim. And again she found legal authority in support, albeit slightly older: since recovery of his car was uncertain - litigation being a lottery - John would have suffered a "loss" within the meaning of the policy.[9]

---

[7]. In the Court of Appeal reported as *Dobson v General Accident Fire and Life Assurance Corp plc* [1989] 3 All England Law Reports 927.

[8]. This time a decision of the House of Lords reported as *National Employers Mutual General Insurance Association Ltd v Jones* [1988] 2 All England Law Reports 425.

[9]. A decision of Mr Justice Parker, not undermined by criticism in later cases, reported as *Webster v General Accident Fire and Life Assurance Corporation Ltd.* [1953] 1 All England Law Reports 663.

Arms did not like this either. He came up to the office to spell out the implications in the real, insurance world.

"You're making us insure fools parted from their money, like insuring against the tide coming in. It means they don't mind being conned and this encourages fraudsters and that's against public policy!"

Putting his arm round her shoulders, he added, caringly:

"Surely a solicitor could get struck off for less - must be conduct unbecoming, eh?"

She smiled widely, whilst contemplating conduct even less becoming but physically more painful, and wriggled away:

"It's down to the Prof, you know, his independent decision and he is my boss."

"Don't give me that, I know what he's like, any half-way pretty girl could twist him round her little finger!"

"If she wanted to, perhaps, but I don't." Charlotte felt half-way pretty angry, near to tears of fury.

Arms left the room, uncaringly and a bit abruptly.

"Good for you, Lot," said Maddie, "the BIG boys think they own us as well as the scheme. But let me try you out with one of mine that's not too different. Punter in a pub sells his Rolex to bloke at the bar, takes a dud cheque for it. . ."

"Rather reckless?" Charlotte interjected.

"It was a good forgery of a building society cheque."

"Alright, borderline winner on same principles."

"But," said Maddie, "the bloke at the bar's our claimant - he paid good money for the cheque and on

CHAPTER FIVE

top of that it was a stolen Rolex. The police none too gently removed it from his wrist, presumably to return it to the true owner. Our bloke was arrested but let off with a caution and is claiming his loss is covered under BIG's famous 'all risks' policy."

"So a trick question, what's the answer?"

"Not an insured peril," Maddie replied, "despite the description, even the thickest of policyholders can't reasonably expect cover for every possible loss."

"I had one like that," said Chip, who had been helping herself uninvited to a complimentary coffee. "Wife called police in the middle of the night to let poor old punter out of the lav - locked himself in, might be dying, she thought - they broke the door down, damaged it beyond repair, but the old boy wasn't there - found the deaf git sound asleep in the spare bedroom. Police were amused but he wasn't, claimed a new door from BIG. Insured peril? Nearest was 'malicious damage', even the Prof didn't think it on!"

"Well the moral must be avoid spare beds and pubs," ventured Charlotte, thinking at least she met one of these.

"Stick to wine bars, eh?" said Maddie. At which point a leer peered round the door:

"Could you spare a moment Ms Angus?" Marian the Manager was crooking a finger. "A word in private, if you please."

Without evincing any enthusiasm, she followed him along to his largish room.

"Mr Scott has just left in a bit of a strop. He's asked me as Clerk to Council to put on the agenda for the next Meeting 'the excessive legalism of recent decisions' - this means you've upset him!"

"Well, what of it, the Ombudsman was happy with them," said Charlotte.

"Don't imagine, just because of Stefano outings, that you're the only iron he's got in the fire. He's frying other fish all the time. Why only this afternoon he spent the best part of an hour on the phone talking to someone called Dorothy, making a date for something special next week."

He leered even more.

"And before you ask, it's my business as General Manager to know what's going on with my staff."

Whose staff? was her thought as she in her turn left abruptly, before tears, only saying sharply:

"So what!"

At reception Sarah smiled up through her phoning, she was copy-typing too, all of which explained a lot.

"Oh yes, it's Sarah at the switch-board telling Marian about our phone calls, but we hadn't actually known she listened in as well. So if you can't be good, better be careful!" Maddie said happily. "I always am - really personal calls, speak in code, so you won't understand, never mind tarty Sarah!"

"Clever," nodded Charlotte, "especially that sporting one: gates open at half-six, kit-off at seven, drinks at half-time, scores at bed-time - what could that be about?"

"Well, it should be too subtle a game for Sarah and outside Marian's playing experience."

Giggles overtook the tears.

CHAPTER FIVE

Later at Stefano's, after the first half bottle, Charlotte felt relaxed enough to ask Ollie a crucial question:

"Who's Dorothy?"

"Dorothy?" he repeated. "Do you mean Dorothea?"

"Might do - Robin was saying something about her organising a special event next week," she said as if explaining.

"Nothing to do with him - it's a public lecture at UCL, my old college, University of London. My father sent me there because it was founded as 'that Godless place in Gower Street.' I got to know Dorothea Copeland as a colleague when I was an Assistant Lecturer at King's, the religious reaction in the Strand. It was my first teaching appointment, just after qualifying as a solicitor nearly 30 years ago. I was paid more then than if I'd stayed with the firm. Unbelievable now - articled clerks do better than lecturers!"

Ollie pondered, perhaps regretting that he had taken the path away from a profitable partnership in practice, before proceeding:

"She's Dr Copeland now, generally known as Thea but everyone called her Dotty then - can't always get away with that nowadays and can't stomach Thea, so it's often Dorothea, easily misheard. PhD in aboriginal site rights, she's UCL's Reader in Proprietorial Philosophies in the Faculty of Law and, in pursuance of further promotion through humouring the Dean, volunteered to run this year's lectures on 'Difficult Lawyers' Concepts'."

"Anyway, would you like to come?" he continued. "Wednesday, food and drinks in the Cloisters after the lecture. Jeremy Bentham should be there, the lecture series is supposed to be in his honour."

"Who is he, exactly," she asked a little resignedly, he was going to tell her whether she asked or not.

"A long-deceased Professor of Jurisprudence, had himself embalmed, sits in a glass box, 18th century clothes, wig and pipe, gets wheeled out for important dinners and meetings, to which he makes an invaluable contribution. If we ever see sense and get rid of the monarchy to have a constitutional presidency, I'd vote for Bentham as President, better brain than Reagan had and just as much use as Bush seems. We only need a symbol and he'd certainly be cheaper to feed and house than the Queen, and he'd perform better - pre-recorded speeches through a loud speaker in his mouth. . ."

"What's the public lecture about?" Charlotte interrupted, trying to halt a run-a-way hobby-horse.

"Reform of Conveyancing, with special reference to contractual formalities and the abolition of gazumping. At least that's what Dotty thinks." Ollie replied.

"And who's the lecturer," she enquired, not instantly enamoured of the subject.

"Me."

Chapter six

Lecture Day

Five-ish, after work on Wednesday, drizzling so much that Charlotte and Ollie took a taxi, despite the short walk, to UCL's Gower Street entrance. Ignoring the splendidly grandiose stairway, which had featured briefly in the *Doctor in the House* film but which actually led to a locked library door opened only to mislead the occasional royal visitors, they entered unobtrusively at the side. Signs indicated where to find the Gustave Tuck lecture theatre. Fortunately, Ollie knew nothing about Tuck to tell her, except that in his undergraduate days the signs had been permanently as well as vulgarly defaced.

Schoolboy humour should stop at school, she thought.

"You'd better go on and wait," said he. "I'll be expected to make an impressive appearance when the audience has assembled - if any, don't bate your breath!"

She found the Tuck theatre up an awkward flight of stairs, near the roof. It was narrow and steep - Ollie had said he would feel like truth at the bottom of a well. It was also unlit and empty. She turned on all the light-switches, not all of which worked but it became a little less gloomy, and sat high up at the back to wait, half hoping it was the wrong place and/or day. However soon a few obvious students began to arrive. Ollie had explained why, they would have been told by straight-faced but hypocritical tutors that the lecture would have 'examination significance'.

"Implication, there'll be a question on the subject and they'll stand a better chance of passing if they've listened to me - but the questions have already been set and no-one, least of all me, knows whether I'll say anything remotely relevant."

The theatre had half filled from the back downwards when, shortly after the 6 o'clock start-time, staff-like beings began entering at the front and distributing themselves apparently according to an order of precedence: the older, the nearer the platform. A number of extremely aged and confident gentlemen - no women - even seated themselves, lastly and noisily, in the very first row facing the lecturer's lectern. Then a surprise, a tall willowy figure from her past slipped into the seat beside Charlotte's: by all that's wonderful, Timmy Lloyd, private eye. She used to instruct him in personal injuries actions to catch out shamming plaintiffs, although she knew he had always preferred divorce work. Their affair had been short but not brutish, their relationship had remained cordial but not close. But -

"What on earth are you doing here?" she whispered.

"Shh, big insurance job," he tapped his nose on one side. Leaving her wondering: big or BIG?

They were whispering because Ollie had just been led on to the platform by Germaine Greer, except that this was actually a similarly handsome black woman. Magnificently middle-aged, close-curled white hair, rose-coloured spectacles, floor length flowery dress, ribbons and beads. The Prof, clad cautiously in charcoal

CHAPTER SIX

grey, sat where indicated and put a thick wad of papers on the table ostentatiously in front of him. Charlotte could feel students groaning and, recalling Cambridge, sympathised.

"Welcome, I am Dr Copeland," the statuesque woman introduced herself from the unnecessarily microphoned lectern, necessarily bathed in a feeble spotlight.

"It is my privilege and also great pleasure to present this evening's most distinguished speaker."

No other speakers then, thought Charlotte.

"As many of you will know, Professor Goodman recently returned to civilisation after several years missionary work north of Watford," she laughed conventionally at her own traditional witticism.

Not Australian, posh English accent but a dash of French, Charlotte diagnosed.

"Seriously though, his special area of research, the implications, iniquitous he would say," - she smiled towards Ollie who surely grimaced - "of the Statute of Frauds 1677 expanded in the seventies - the 1970s - to embrace critical studies of successive Solicitors Acts. The publications emerging from his researches made him widely known in expert circles as a campaigning advocate for the abolition of any legal requirements that the purchase of real property should involve written documents or indeed qualified conveyancers. His two texts entitled in his inimitable style *Everything Oral* and *Be Your Own Solicitor* attracted appropriate attention and, I'm told, sold well in the States for a while. And deservedly - reviewed in the Law Quarterly together with a number of other potentially popular booklets, the eminent editor identified these two pamphlets as 'the least practical'. High academic commendation from such a source, as you will all appreciate! Once a graduate at this College and now an Honorary Professor of this University, I can conceive of no better person to address today's topic: *Reform of Conveyancing*, notwithstanding his current close concerns with the insurance market. Professor Goodman."

They'll all think he's now an insurance salesman and want to know his commission, thought Charlotte, angry and amused.

Desultory clapping accompanied Ollie as he sidled towards the lectern. Edging behind Dr Copeland he disappeared from sight, then reappeared clambering back onto the platform only to disappear again behind the lectern. Reappearing around the side, holding the microphone, he said, seeming to smile through his teeth:

"Thank you so much for that fulsomely selective introduction. In the time remaining to me, I shall certainly try to address as many aspects of your chosen topic as possible."

Turning to the auditorium, the Prof began: "Ladies and gentlemen, members of the public, members of the professions and members of the Faculty."

That insult was perhaps a touch too subtle, thought Charlotte.

"When Dotty, sorry Dr Copeland invited me to deliver a lecture in this prestigious series, I was not so

CHAPTER SIX

much honoured as astonished. After all she has heard me lecture before. Ha ha! However when I was appointed as insurance ombudsman, media training was arranged for me - like the remuneration something beyond the comprehension of most academics. The essential thing, I learnt, was to get your own message across. So whatever an interviewer asked, the answer should begin: 'yes, but the real issue is. . .' The first question at my first television interview was could I say a few words about the future of the insurance industry. Viewers may have been surprised to receive several words on conveyancing reform. Now the boot is on the other foot. But don't despair, the topics are related - Her Majesty's Land Registry should properly be treated as little more than a specialist insurance company ripe for development!"

"Dotty, Dr Copeland," - Charlotte caught the calculated stutter-effect - "well knows that experienced speakers rarely read papers, preferring to speak to the topic thus allowing listeners to concentrate on primary principles before perusing the details later at leisure. I am no exception - my paper will be published in due course."

Ollie gestured at the wad of papers placed prominently on the table. It was subsequently discovered that he had, no doubt inadvertently, brought a collection of copy decision letters recently issued by the office. His paper was never, to Charlotte's knowledge, seen by anyone.

"It is a matter of history that the solicitors' profession strongly opposed the idea of any registration of title system when it was proposed towards the end of the 19th century. This opposition was not simply the practitioner's knee-jerk reaction to change - old dogs don't want to learn new tricks. Nor was it solely because the scale fees for registered conveyancing would be lower than for unregistered. No, they were not stupid, they saw and feared the real idea: registration of title was designed to enable ordinary people to do their own conveyancing!"

"The vendor and the purchaser would go together to the Land Registry and over a counter the vendor's name would be examined and crossed off the register and, on payment of the price, the purchaser's name entered. All done then and there, no contracts, no gazumping or gazundering, and no solicitors' bills. The plan was to open a registry office in every town, amalgamating it with existing registers - births, deaths, marriages and titles, - not necessarily in that order. Ha! Ha! Came to nothing, of course, not easy to take the bread and butter out of an old dog's mouth."

"So we still have a Land Registry, run by solicitors for solicitors," the Prof pressed on. "Pretends to be about land ownership, but in reality does not guarantee ownership itself but merely offers to indemnify the person registered as owner if the register turns out to be wrong and his name removed. Worse, this insurance, for that's essentially what it is, expressly does not cover a whole host of hostile rights called 'overriding interests' - tenants' rights, squatters, beneficiaries can all come out of the woodwork, not an insured peril says HM Land Registry. Small print exclusion clauses!"

CHAPTER SIX

At this point there was a disturbance - not a protest from the Chief Land Registrar who had heard it all before, but a cry for help from someone in the front row.

"It's alright," called Ollie, "it's only the Sub-Dean."

He proceeded to explain for the benefit of the audience:

"Fell asleep, toppled against the Dean, disturbed one of his dreams, but he knows where he is now, poor old chap. Reminds me of dreaming I was lecturing on equity and trusts, woke up, found I was. Ha! Ha! Sleeping in an upright position was learnt as a vital skill when I was student, attendance at lectures being compulsory. Sub-Dean's probably an Oxbridge graduate, never attended any lectures!"

Not just the students were sniggering. Staff chuckled discreetly and even Charlotte was tickled.

"If you're all settled comfortably, I'll continue," said Ollie happily. "I'm about to be in serious breach of the Official Secrets Act. Information has reached my ear - reliable source, only disclosed for suitable consideration - that next on the Prime Minister's list for privatisation is, you guessed it, the Land Registry. Seems something annoyed Maggie when she moved to No.10, perhaps they would only register her with a possessory title! Ha! Ha!"

"The banks and building societies, not to mention insurance companies, are very excited. Hailsham led them to expect a cut of the conveyancing cake in 1984 but reneged. Now if they get their hands on the Land Registry, they can expand its customer services, reinvent the original idea, replace the solicitors' monopoly with their own, extend the insurance cover, not just 'overriding interests' but the whole household, building and contents, underwritten at proper premiums naturally. There would be fantastic opportunities for marketing financial products to a captive customer base already hooked on endowment mortgages. You know, of course, about modern mortgages - a weapon of warfare, kills the people but leaves the buildings standing!"

"The reform of conveyancing will not depend on lawyers but will be driven by market forces," Ollie pronounced politically as well as oratorically.

Does he believe any of this? wondered Charlotte. He went on to what she knew he did believe in:

"Naturally, although self-regulation should prove satisfactory, some controls will still be needed to placate the consumer protection lobby and to afford a measure of credibility to the industry's codes of conduct. Co-incidentally," he observed disingenuously, "the Government is already reviewing existing provisions for there to be a 'conveyancing ombudsman' for authorised practitioners. Not yet implemented, but the time is ripening and, if it is, I shall stand - ready, able and willing!"

So proclaiming, the Prof stepped back from the lectern and fell off the platform.

"Oh! Darling!" shrieked Dr Copeland.

"That's my girl. That's what I want to hear," muttered Timmy.

I don't, thought Charlotte.

CHAPTER SIX

Then the Prof clambered back onto the platform, showing no signs of suffering any injury from his fall, to receive much greater applause than ever during the lecture. Dotty hugged him and the applause increased. Still hugging, she turned to the auditorium:

"Shall we all repair to the Cloisters for medicinal drinks? Such a stimulating talk, stunned into silence, no questions here but Oliver, that is Professor Goodman will be available there to conduct discussions, in private of course."

Not too privately, I trust, was Charlotte's thought.

"Come, Jeremy Bentham awaits us!"

Timmy had already slipped away. Staff and distinguished visitors, then students and others, including Charlotte, followed Dr Copeland as she woman-handled Ollie down the stairs. Crushed to one side at the near end of the Cloisters which ran the length of the College's main building, Charlotte reached the reception, pushed through drinkers to trestle tables.

"Red, white, juice or water?" she was asked.

She took a glass of white wine and looked for Ollie whilst listening to the chatter. Someone was saying:

"Up North he was known as 'Superprof', I was told he used to give lectures stripped to the waist - until his legs got cold!"

Another remarked: "Granada had him fronting a series of DIY programmes on conveyancing - peak-time viewing, 9.30 Sunday mornings, seen by literally tens of people!"

And another: "He kept video recordings of the programmes for his seminar groups to watch while he drank coffee and read *The Times*."

But another: "At least he practises what he preaches - done his own conveyancing every time he's moved house - so he knows what it's like to get a defective title!"

Jeremy Bentham, over by the wall neglected in his box, beamed at them all but not benignly. Timmy, glass in hand still full, was studying an explanatory plaque on the box, oblivious apparently to all around.

Charlotte spotted Ollie in close conversation with Dr Copeland. No-one else was near. Pariahs or private discussions? She wondered. Snatching a hot sausage roll from a passing tray-bearer, she invaded their privacy, or pariahdom. Feeling feeble, she sought notice with:

"Hello."

"Oh there you are," shouted himself, obviously over-excited. "Don't tell me what you thought of the show - I'm easily offended! Ha! Ha! Dorothea, darling, meet Charlotte Angus, the brilliant lawyer I was telling you about, working for us now, God knows why, we pay her barely more than a lecturer!"

Her hand was grasped, squashing the sausage roll.

"Ow! That was hot! Call me Thea. How do you put up with him? I've spent years trying to put him down - not succeeded yet!"

Charlotte could think of nothing brilliant to say, so she laughed which seemed to suffice for Thea and asked Ollie:

"Are you really alright?"

"They'll have thought I was drunk," said the hero of the moment, drinking up his red wine instead of

Chapter Six

answering.

"If he wasn't drunk then, about which I have profound doubts," Thea interposed, "he soon will be."

"Purely anaesthetic, little pain, bruises perhaps, used to play rugger, lecturing usually less dangerous," said he quietly, adding loudly: "Dean must expect me to sue - could be debilitating complications."

"Only from inebriation or, if anyone took you seriously, retaliation," chuckled a little brown man with smiley eyes and a square jaw. "Well done, your usual performance, thought-provoking as always."

"Certainly aroused a few of those physically present," observed Thea pointedly.

The little man chuckled on unabashed.

"Lot, let me introduce Professor Copeland, for his sins not only Dean of the Faculty but also Dorothea's unfortunate husband. Roy meet my legal assistant, Charlotte Angus."

"Delighted my dear," the Dean dodged her sausage-rolly hand, and turned back to the Prof: "But Oliver whatever happened to the charming young lady you brought a couple of years ago? Wasn't she your, uh, legal assistant?"

"That was no lady, that was Maddie, ha ha! - I remember she asked if you got your suntan holidaying in the West Indies and whether Dotty wore long dresses to hide her fat legs. Nor was she legal. She's still with us, but as for College do's - tried it once, didn't like it!"

"Thea dear, we must circulate. Oliver, one evening soon dinner?" said the Dean, taking his lady's arm firmly, she adding:

85

"Yes, before too long, while you're still alone in London. Charlotte could come too. I'll ring you."

They left to join their colleagues, hints sown for a legal assistant to reap if she wished.

"Time to do an Irish runner," said Ollie. "I know an escape route."

"Why 'Irish'?" asked Charlotte.

"Because I've already paid."

He led her back towards the stairs leading up to the Gustave Tuck lecture theatre, saying loudly as they passed his erstwhile audience:

"The loos are this way".

"Don't get lost again," someone called out.

Dotty, thought Charlotte appreciating the ambiguity.

They descended to a basement-level side entrance suitable for students and tradesman, walked between refuse bins, cycle racks and discarded packing cases, under arches, pipes and conduits, exiting across from Dillon's bookshop. Ollie had seemed, to Charlotte, suspiciously confident of the route.

"The Faculty was on this corner over a chemist's when I started," he said. "No big bookshop, no students' union, just a bar in the basement - ah, the good old days!"

Chapter Seven

Spag Night

"Where are you taking me?" Charlotte doubted the honourability of his intentions as well as the reliability of the route. She could not see Timmy Lloyd watching as if a guardian angel, camcorder in lieu of sword.

"Thought we might have a bite to eat, if you've time."

It was still only twenty past seven - the last train to Chelmsford ran much later, as he undoubtedly knew.

"OK," she said, to his obvious surprise.

"What about the Spag House?" he proposed. "Handy for Holborn and I lust after their *spezzatino* - beef stew to you. Or actually my flat's only in Gray's Inn Road, no problem to serve up pasta, cheese and wine, if you prefer."

Not just stew he's lusting after, Charlotte thought but:

"I shouldn't be too late to-night," she said inappropriately. "They'll be expecting me reasonably early," she added untruthfully. "A quickish snack at the Spaghetti House would probably be better," she concluded - regretfully? She wondered. "Perhaps another time when I've warned them not to expect me," she heard herself say, promisingly.

The first pass, not caught nor dropped but fumbled.

Retracing on foot their taxi route from the office, they passed the Tavistock Hotel.

"Stayed there for a few nights when I first came to London," said Ollie. "No ambiance, but perfectly adequate for short stays. Before I bought the flat - Gray's Inn Road, it's straight on here," he added with optimistic persistence.

"Right, I think," said Charlotte, missing a second pass not too sharply. "Southampton Row up to the Spaghetti House."

"Been eating there for years, not pretentious, cheap and cheerful like us, convenient for business lunches" - and for developing personnel relationships at other times, neither said. "There's still a staircase straight from the office into the middle of the restaurant, not used now, except as a fire escape. Remember when I was first appointed, the office-boy wanted a specimen signature, felt important, thought it was for the bank account, but no I'm not trusted with that, it was for the office account with the Spag House!"

"Ah Professor Oliver, welcome, and the beautiful signorina," they were greeted by a tall, dark and amiable manager. "Through here as usual?"

He led the way past the kitchen.

"See the fire escape," whispered Ollie.

Waiters and waitresses smiled welcomingly. They sat facing each other, comparatively inconspicuously, at the narrow end of the room, their view through the windows mostly obscured by hanging plants and bottles, all green. Timmy Lloyd, looking in from the pavement if he passed from time to time, would not disturb them. A bottle of Antinori Chianti Classico arrived apparently unordered. Instead of stew - no lusts were to be satisfied

Chapter Seven

that evening - both had tagliatelle with a spicy sausage sauce and shared a joke about her earlier hot-squashed-roll.

"The idea that I could drink enough of the Faculty's vile plonk to get drunk was probably the worst insult of the evening," mused Ollie.

"So far," said Charlotte.

"Oh this red is always very drinkable," demonstrating his point as he let her point escape him.

They ate for a while in silence. Then, feeling emboldened by the wine and enabled by his passes, Charlotte broke open her 'wanna-knows'.

"Alright, Ollie, question time. Your starter for anything, what's Dorothea to you?"

"We're just bad friends," he replied. "I told you, thirty years ago, both Assistant Lecturers at King's competing for promotion. Got on well, she was brilliant and beautiful, popular with staff and students. But with blatant discrimination, another dull chap and I were made Lecturers. She had to leave. Sought fame and fortune in the colonies - Jamaica, no joke. We'd got on well as junior colleagues, flirted a bit but nothing developed and at King's staff didn't meet casually over coffee in the Faculty. It was extremely primitive then, rooms above a greengrocer's shop on the Strand reached via an outside wooden staircase. The College itself still had a 'Men's Senior Common Room' - women not admitted. Remember Rosie in *Double Helix*, the DNA story, killed her! Dotty married Roy in 1985, after he'd been a Visiting Professor in the West Indies, where he was born and where she'd become a Senior Lecturer.

Cynics say she bought a ticket back to the UK, certainly he brought his bag and baggage with him when he became Dean. Sort of 'quid pro-motion', ha ha! We'd met at odd Conferences over the years, she'd never married before but I never got anywhere with her - not that I was really trying, of course," he added hastily.

"Of course not," Charlotte agreed.

"Never forgave me for the unfair promotion. Anyway when she got back to London I turned out to be the only old friend still around. Family's all in Mauritius, French speaking, she hardly hears from them. Hence the continuing contact with me. Roy's intensely jealous, understandable perhaps, but without cause and she gets on like a house on fire with Beryl."

"That's your second question, for a bonus if you're lucky," Charlotte interrupted. "What about your wife?"

Ollie for once was thinking before speaking.

"Take your time," she said.

"What about pudding?" he enquired, saved by a waiter offering desserts. "I can recommend the figs. Keeps one regular."

Take more than a fig to regularise you, she thought, but looked at her watch saying:

"No just a cappuccino, please."

"Same for me," said Ollie to the waiter.

When the coffee had come, she said:

"Now go on, you've had enough time."

"We met in 1967, married in 1968. Five years older than me - took my age but not my name on marriage! She'd spent a couple of years in the States establishing a formidable reputation as an International Lawyer,

Chapter Seven

although her thesis was never published, appointed with acclaim, she demonstrated her superior intellect by abrasive wit, especially in meetings - 'point of order, Mr Chairman' was her feared war-cry. She was not unattractive then and the brainiest eligible female in the Faculty, not that there was much competition. So one thing led too far too fast. It was alright for a few years - except actually on the physical side which never really worked."

Ollie fell silent for a while before, apparently, explaining something:

"We've always had quite a few interests in common, teaching as well as theatre and such like, but especially holidaying in France. Me for the food and drink, she for culture. So in the earlier '70s she started going to evening classes in 'advanced French conversation', then she took GCE O-level French - A-grade, needless to say. These were all adult classes taken by a primary school teacher who treated her pupils as naughty children, whatever their age and status, and I rather got the idea that that was what Beryl really liked about it. However in no time at all she was specialising in Comparative French Law and introducing degree courses on Law and French involving a term a year at the University of Bordeaux."

"You'd have enjoyed that," Charlotte interjected. "Exchange students, not all male, and plenty of claret-tasting opportunities!"

"True enough to begin with, but the fun went out of France for me - holidays have become work, serious research, no R-and-R, sights and sites to be seen."

"Hardly grounds for divorce," she was unimpressed.

"Unreasonable behaviour?" he suggested. "Some of mine may have been! Probably not, but enough for leave of absence from each other, on compassionate grounds. Weekend visiting doesn't strain our relationship, leaves us free to pursue our own interests and lets us live separately while keeping up appearances."

"And you pursue other women?"

"No, no, that's not what I meant, she's never objected to that - not that there was any of that, at least not to speak of - the last straw was her refusal to play bridge with me any more!"

"Gosh, that is serious," Charlotte was not serious. "So you've had to give up playing?"

"Well no," Ollie was serious, "but I had to find another suitable partner, not easy."

"Lucky at cards. . .?" she wondered aloud, but this was not thought amusing.

"Found someone to play with at the Law Commission, actually they found me, needed a fourth for lunch times. Their office is opposite Gray's Inn, just along Theobald's Road, we play there once a week but once a month they come to me."

"So that explains the breaches of your open-door policy."

"They don't like coming, having to leave the spacious comfort of their own offices and then endure Mrs Arden's severe disapproval!"

"And your new partner, is he a suitable substitute for your spouse?" asked Charlotte, guessing the answer.

"Ah! Ann's a barrister in the civil service."

CHAPTER SEVEN

I knew it, she thought.

"She's stronger than me, more experienced at least and, before you ask, there's nothing else between us. We play bridge together, lunchtimes and some evenings - a few matches and a club night. That's all."

"Married?"

"Not yet, but believed to be courting - one of the Parliamentary Counsel seconded to the Law Commission, a non-bridge player to our surprise," Ollie sounded shifty she thought.

"OK, let's move on to your last question, for the jackpot perhaps," Oops, the second bottle of Chianti's talking, she thought, but she asked anyway: "Where does Maddie fit into your life?"

"Nowhere in the sense you have in mind," Ollie protested. "She was the only assistant three years ago, we were both unattached during the week so naturally I took her out a few times."

"No naughtiness?" Would his version match Maddie's?

"Well there was a little flame for a while, then it flickered out, by mutual agreement not worth relighting. She's amazing but not in ways I could live with and being amazed all the time is very tiring. We're not close any more, in fact there were hostilities for a while, but now there's a sort of truce or at least cease-fire and I wouldn't be without her in the office. She's with someone else now, rumour has it, from Lloyd's - able to afford her, I expect!"

Matches sufficiently, she decided to herself, but not to-night Oliver.

"Getting late, must go," Charlotte announced.

"Dare I ask you anything similarly personal?" Ollie queried, uncharacteristically tentative.

She wondered what she should say, then: "Marriage not too secure - caught Simon 'up to no good' - tit-for-tat crossed my mind."

"Sauce for the gander, eh Lottie?"

"Yes that sort of thing and you're willing to be goose, eh Ollie?"

"When or if you're sure, not before."

Too true, she thought but then conceded something significant, to her at least: "You can call me Lot, in private."

He escorted her to the Holborn Tube with good grace but no further. She thanked him with honest sincerity for a fascinating evening, even complimenting him on his terrific lecture, and offered her cheek for a farewell kiss. Which he properly gave, without holding her by the shoulders, and they said 'goodnight', 'see you to-morrow', neither mentioning but both holding hopes and ideas for the future. His was a short walk to the flat and a little loneliness, hers a run to catch the last train to Chelmsford and a quasi-happy family. That Timmy Lloyd followed him not her, disappointedly, she could not have noticed.

Chapter Eight

Cases Continued

Next morning Maddie greeted her with: "How'd it go last night? I bet he scored!"

Charlotte had anticipated this line of questioning and decided upon a straight-faced pose: "His lecture was well received, despite a certain lack of *gravitas*, as intellectually stimulating with practical implications of importance…"

"Yeh, yeh! He had 'em rolling in the aisles, as always, but what about last night - all I want to know is did he roll you over and into bed?"

"Don't be so vulgar! We had a meal downstairs in the Spag House and I then went home alone to my own bed," in the spare bedroom, Charlotte did not add. On her return, prepared to explain the late hour with plausible details of College functions, she had found the twins asleep like angels and her spouse snoring like a pig. Nanny Rosa's room had been dark and quiet - dealing daily with Danny and Benjy, as she well knew, would exhaust anyone.

"Alright, alright," said Maddie. "Better luck next time - him not you I mean! He'll try again, we all know he fancies you something rotten. And you do spend all that quality time together at Stefano's."

However Charlotte had learnt a little of her roommate's witty repartee and, quick as a flash, replied:

"Shut your face!"

"Ignore her," said Ollie arriving for his coffee and over-hearing. It was not apparent which of them he was advising. "All ready for the show?" he continued contentedly, "you might find this interesting. . . Lot," the pause seemed significant, "after lunch - Maddie has the file." He departed drinking dangerously from his cup.

"What's he talking about?" demanded Charlotte.

"Ill-health cover, punter suffered back injury lifting crates of beer for a party last Christmas, claimed 'permanent total disablement from all gainful employment' - Arms's nose twitched and he set a private detective on him."

"Which one did he use?" asked Charlotte, suddenly looking for a 2 to put together with another.

"Oh, Timothy Lloyd Associates, always uses them, usually reliable although they did once report on the wrong brother, looked alike! Anyway, in this case there's not only a report but also a video showing the claim up as fraudulent - the nose strikes again!"

"So what's the problem?" Charlotte asked.

"Arms has refused to let the punter see the evidence in case the claim goes to court - says the punter might tailor his story. Not surprisingly the punter's stuck to his guns and appealed to the Prof - he's frightened of prosecution, Arms always threatens people with the police, and he thinks this appeal proves his innocence, otherwise why would he be appealing? The Prof, putting it politely, regards Arms's attitude as unconstructive and has issued an ultimatum - show up or pay up. So

CHAPTER EIGHT

the punter's coming in this afternoon to watch the video, see the evidence against him and have an opportunity of explaining it away. Arms will be here too, so with any luck there might be a punch up. Should be fun!" Maddie rubbed her hands happily.

That afternoon, the punter, Ronald Rattee, limped painfully into the so-called Council Chamber. A TV set and video recorder had been installed at one end of the table, borrowed, Maddie said, from Marian the Manager's room:

"He's nothing better to do and loves children's telly."

Mr Rattee's use of his sticks was awkward and, at Ollie's invitation, he lowered himself into a seat with obvious difficulty. Arms sat opposite glowering. Ollie between them enquired caringly:

"Your wife?"

"Couldn't come."

"Your car?"

"Public transport."

"Very well," Ollie continued. "This is Mr Scott from BIG, the insurers; Ms Hill and Ms Angus are my assistants. We've going to watch the evidence on which BIG relies in declining your claim. Only Mr Scott has seen it so far. Then we should understand BIG's position and can talk about what should happen sensibly. Alright?"

"OK, go ahead," said Roland Rattee resignedly.

Ollie nodded to Maddie standing as if the grim executioner of his ombudsmanic orders beside the TV and video.

Maddie pressed the ON button and retired hastily to sit with Charlotte at the other end of the room behind

Love At All Risks

and to each side of Ollie. Their files had been crammed, Charlotte's carefully, beneath the table.

Ollie said: "I'll turn the lights off, then," and did so.

As he sat down, everyone quiet, Mr Rattee was seen on the screen: the shot was time-dated - Friday 13 January 1989 - and he was running, wearing overalls, for a bus which he caught, jumping aboard easily swinging a bag of tools in one hand. Later he was seen alighting, without difficulty, and walking rapidly up to a scaffolded house. He climbed quickly up a ladder carrying his bag in one hand. Then he took a heavy hammer out of the bag and began to hit things on the roof. After this there was very little plot development of any interest but many sightings of Ronald the able-bodied roofer until, seemingly responding to a summons, he descended the ladder quickly and entered the house hastily through the front door, closed behind him by a lady.

A break in recording was followed by a scene through a window: naked bodies on a bed. Arms pressed the pause button on a remote control.

"What follows may not be suitable viewing with ladies present," he said.

Maddie and Charlotte looked at each other, eyebrows raised.

"Thank you Mr Scott," Ollie said. "What do you think of the show so far Mr Rattee?"

After a long while, Roland the video-star said: "That was one of my good days."

After which explanation he stood up and left the room.

Ollie called after him: "You've forgotten your sticks."

Chapter Eight

But he did not look back.

"You will report him, won't you?" said Arms.

"What to his wife?" Ollie asked.

"No, to the police or Social Security, he should be prosecuted, he's a bloody crook," insisted Arms.

"Of course not," came the principled reply. "No policyholder should be worse off as a result of appealing to the Ombudsman."

"Alright, I'll turn the bugger in myself," Arms said, leaving the room holier, and angrier, than ordinary mortals.

"And we can watch the rest of the video," crowed Maddie, turning to the TV, still paused on naked bodies. Ron the rat was not only able-bodied but well underwritten. But not technically a bugger. Nonetheless, his disablement claim extremely plainly failed.

Third file - the Case of the Broken Brokers

Having retrieved her piles of files from their hiding-place under the table, Charlotte returned to work. Six comparative quickies, the first infuriating Arms and Fingers because it amounted to 'law reform by the back door'.

Maddie had explained the background. Like other insurers, BIG sold its policies through brokers and other 'independent intermediaries'. These gentlemen present proposal forms and suggest policies for all the world as if salesmen employed by the insurer which would pay them by means of commission on sales. But in law this was a trap for the unwary: the long-established legal position is that a broker acts as the policyholder's agent, not the insurer's. So if the broker made a mistake about what the policy covered, the insurer could escape liability. Or if the broker failed to pass on material information, the insurer could avoid the policy for non-disclosure.

At first sight, and prejudiced by Maddie's version, this rule seemed not a little inequitable to Charlotte.[10] So she looked it up in the books and discovered that as long ago as 1957 the Law Reform Committee had recommended a new rule: any person who solicits or negotiates a contract of insurance should be deemed to be the insurer's agent. This recommendation had never been implemented but Ollie agreed with her - he seemed to think that agreeing with her might save time - that he should apply the rule anyway as being 'fair and reasonable'. The fact that this enlightened, consumer-friendly criterion was permitted by the Ombudsman's terms of reference was something BIG's boys were coming to appreciate less and less.

Accordingly, in a case where a so-called independent financial adviser had concealed the early surrender penalty when misselling a life policy, Ollie and Charlotte made BIG repay the premiums. Fingers objected of course, but not for as long as expected, partly because he could recover the commission paid and partly because the loss would not affect shareholders, only

---

10. As indeed it had, very recently, to Lord Justice Purchas who thought it "remarkable" that a broker "who is remunerated by the insurance industry and who presents proposal forms and suggested policies on their behalf" should be treated as agent of the policy holder. This observation was made in a case reported as *Roberts v Plaisted* [1989] 2 Lloyd's Law Reports 341.

other policyholders. He even attempted a joke, not in the best of taste, about the IFA who had sold a policy to Salman Rushdie without warning him of the 'fatwah' exclusion. Charlotte smiled politely whilst wondering about BIG's own policies - they tended not to cover 'Acts of God' nor, since the IRA visited London, the activities of terrorists.

Fourth file - the Case of the Dodgy Lodger

Charlotte picked up another file from the floor. More back door law reform? she wondered.

Pensioner Jack Lindsay had bought a big house in Brighton for his and his wife's retirement and insured it against fire with BIG. The house duly burnt down but BIG declined to pay. Jack had revealed to BIG's loss adjuster that his wife used to earn a little extra through seasonal bed and breakfasting.

"Ah ha, got ya!" cried Arms, "an undisclosed business use - grounds for declinature!"

And strictly in law he was right, Charlotte knew: policyholders have a duty to disclose any fact which a prudent insurer might think material; the slightest breach of this duty entitles repudiation of the policy - premium repayable but all claims rejectable. It was nothing to the point that the fire occurred out of season, not remotely due to B-n-B'ing. Nor was it relevant that Jack's non-disclosure had been innocent - even Arms's nose smelt nothing fishy.

Again this rule of law struck Charlotte as a touch or two too Draconian, neither fair nor reasonable either generally or, more importantly, in the particular case. Again she looked it up in the books and discovered that legislative modifications had been proposed, this time by the Law Commission in 1980, again not implemented. She read the proposals and also considered certain mitigating Statements of Practice issued by the insurers' trade association whilst lobbying successfully against implementation. In her view, none of these were satisfactory.

She consulted Ollie and, surprise surprise, his French connections supplied a suitable solution: proportionality. Jack had paid a premium of £1000; had BIG known of the B-n-B use, it would have charged £1250. In France, not too far from Brighton, the friendly and flexible, if rough and ready law would mean that BIG should pay 80% of Jack's claim. A sufficiently equitable outcome, she thought, contentedly.

Fifth file - the Case of the Smug Smuggler

Charlotte's next file involved fishy facts and fishier law. The story she read seemed to her interesting but Maddie told her it was common-place.

Nicky Pumfrey had been mugged, stripped of his leather jacket and relieved of his Rolex.

"Punters always lose rollers," said Maddie. "Never a Timex!"

"Bought 'em in New York, din' I?" he had explained. "Long week-end away from the missus," and he had produced what purported to be the purchase papers. Where was the receipt for customs duty, he had been

CHAPTER EIGHT

asked.

"Nah, wore 'em through, din' I?" he further explained.

"Oh what a shame! So sorry, but that's criminal," he had been told. "Against public policy to pay you."

"Sure that's right, read the decision in *Geismar v Sun Alliance* decided ten years ago - one of my favourite judgments," said Arms happily.

Sounds like his bedtime reading, thought Charlotte as she went off to find a report of the *Geismar* decision.[11] Mr G had taken out three policies of household insurance. Certain articles were, he claimed, stolen from him and his claim form listed the countries where each of those articles had been purchased, the date of purchase and the price paid. He had imported them without declaring them, he had freely admitted to Sun Alliance's loss adjuster, adding that he never intended to pay customs duty if he could avoid it. Neither the claim nor the confession was disputed.

"In the industry it's widely believed that this was a put-up case, supported by other insurers and with a co-operative claimant, fixed to find another loop-hole to let them off paying, especially for allegedly stolen jewellery," Maddie told her. "Worked brilliantly!"

Indeed it did, Charlotte realised. Although accepting that the policies were not themselves tainted with any illegality, a first instance judge had been persuaded to hold that: "where there is a deliberate breach of the law I do not think a court ought to assist the plaintiff to

---

11. It was reported as *Geismar v Sun Alliance and London Insurance Ltd* [1977] 3 All England Law Reports 570 and widely believed, given the lack of factual disputes, to have been a put-up job on behalf of the insurance industry.

derive a profit from it, even though it is sought indirectly through an indemnity under an insurance policy."

She could certainly understand why Arms liked the decision. However he became much less happy when Charlotte, and then Ollie, expressed a different and rather unfavourable view of the decision. They thought it put insurers into an unacceptably unethical position: it was alright for them to take premiums with no intention of paying claims if they could avoid doing so, but not for others to adopt the same attitude to otherwise due payments. Of course convicted - or confessed - criminals can expect no mercy from insurers but what about the rest? Policyholders, like other citizens, should surely be presumed innocent of smuggling until proven guilty and trap questions calling for self-incrimination without warning ought not to be asked.

"They'll be asking punters about inheritance tax and VAT next," spluttered Ollie, "Or rejecting car claims because the road tax is a little late!"

Nor would he let BIG deduct unpaid duty from the claim: insurers are not tax collectors.

So lucky Nicky won.

Sixth file - the Case of the Furious Fiancé

The next file revealed a sad story, one that was novel not only to Charlotte but also to her cynical colleagues. It also raised a novel point of law.

Andie Park had proposed to Janet Smith, she had

given her hand and taken his ring. Then he had proposed to BIG - for an insurance policy on her life. But was it valid, did unmarried couples have an insurable interest in each other's lives? A nice point of law, turning on a proper construction of the Life Assurance Act of 1774. Oh heartless BIG not to pay! But this was not a deceased darling scenario. No, Janet had jilted Andie and he simply wanted his premium back - and his ring but that was not down to BIG. Fingers was refusing repayment because BIG had been 'on risk', but was he right?

The law seemed completely unclear, so Charlotte turned to practice. She consulted Mount. That large lady was noisily appalled by the very idea that any insurer, even the least reputable, would ever seek to repudiate liability on the death of an insured fiancée. After all, marriage is not as fashionable as it used to be and 'engaged' couples live together more and more in co owned and co-mortgaged properties: if the endowment policies backing the mortgages turned out to be unreliable, the institutional lenders would all be seriously concerned. Satisfied, therefore, that in reality Fingers was not deceiving her by asserting that BIG had been 'on risk', Charlotte concluded that it would be neither fair nor reasonable to require return of the premium. Fingers' astonished appreciation, if nothing else, was touching.

Seventh file - the Case of the Woeful Wife

The following file involved a story that no-one thought novel, not even Charlotte, but the facts seemed sadder and the solution fairer.

In contrast to the briefly engaged couple, Raphael and Rebecca Jacob were married and naturally joint owners of the matrimonial home and its contents all of which property they had wisely - and jointly - insured with BIG. Sadly they had separated and, distressed by her husband's desertion, as she saw it, Rebecca had set fire to the house, destroying everything in it. In due course, Raphael's claim to be indemnified against damage caused by fire had been rejected by BIG.

Charlotte certainly understood this rejection: the damage had been deliberately caused by a policyholder. But the result seemed out of touch with modern thinking - a man and his woman were not one person, husbands were no longer supposed to keep dangerous wives at their peril. So Raphael was eventually held able by the Ombudsman to recover for the loss of his half share: equity is equality. Arms, of course, muttered mainly about rights of subrogation against Rebecca but nobody listened, least of all her. She had killed herself.

Eighth file - the Case of the Missing Spouse

Charlotte picked up another file telling a tale of matrimonial disaster and wondered how her own domestic straights would compare if seen through an insurance company's claims manager.

Percy Rimer had disappeared, leaving clothes and a suicide note on the beach - Hove actually, although completely coincidentally he had spent his last night at Jack's B-n-B in Brighton. Wendy Rimer, grieving as a

CHAPTER EIGHT

widow should, claimed on her policy insuring his life. BIG would not pay: Fingers did not need a sensitive nose to smell a Stonehouse. And once more he was right - Percy had not drowned. But three years later it was established beyond doubt that he had died that night - car crash, in hospital, different identity. He was definitely cheating, but on Wendy, not on BIG. His secretary-mistress confessed all - to a well-known Sunday paper.

Wendy, had also claimed for the car, hers, stolen she thought but actually written-off in the crash that killed Percy. BIG ultimately admitted both claims, for the life and the car, but then interest became the issue. Arms was adamant that general insurers never paid interest on late payments - if they did premiums would have to go up. Fingers on the other hand accepted without difficulty that good insurance practice required life insurers to add interest from, at the latest, two months after death until payment.

Charlotte predictably felt Fingers' to be the better practice. So in support she searched for and found a 1965 judgment where a court had exercised its discretion to award interest on the basis that the policy proceeds really belonged to the policyholder who "could have made as good use of the money which is in issue as could the insurance company." So looking on that as done which ought to have been done, she assumed the claims paid when made and that Wendy would have immediately deposited the money safely with a Building Society and, with the Ombudsman's ready agreement, awarded an appropriately approximate after tax rate.

"Never mind the merits, although they seemed clear enough to me," she crowed to Ollie at Stefano's, "it was worth the hassle to see Arms the claims man and Fingers the money man arguing with each other instead of with us!"

"General insurers and life insurers don't understand each other," mused Ollie, "that still surprises me. I suppose it's long-term and short-term - if Arms' side doesn't like our decisions or suffers more claims than they bargained for, they simply re-write the policies or up the premiums the following year, or both, whereas with Fingers' side the policies are not annual and they feel locked-in, but so are the policyholders, of course."

He took a reflective drink. "Do you feel locked-in … Lot?"

She took a reflective drink. "Have done," she said, "but I feel like escaping now."

"What's happened?" he sounded apprehensive.

He'll be wondering whether something between us is beginning or ending, she thought, which does he fear?

"Yesterday evening we had a row, Simon and me. I told him I was Ms Angus in the office and he didn't like it. Said I was undermining our marriage. Well I wasn't taking that, not after what he'd been up to. So heated words were exchanged, as they say. Until I went too far, screaming insults, sticking my chin out, and he hit me."

She was crying, tears covering her cheeks and dripping on her blouse. He touched her arm tentatively: "Oh my dear," he said uselessly.

Chapter Eight

"First time. Slapped my face. The twins saw." Sobbing made her speech uncontrollably staccato.

"So astonished, then furious, didn't know what to do. Stormed out, walked around the park at the back for hours, in the dark! When I went back he was still up, terribly contrite. Never happen again, etc. etc. But I'm glad really. We couldn't go on as we were."

Ollie murmured "I'm so sorry," without conviction, and offered her his handkerchief which she needed.

"This may not be a good time," Ollie obviously hoped otherwise, "but I had been meaning to ask if you'd like to come to a tasting, Solicitors' Wine Society, pretentious tradesmen, but it's a Chateau Figeac vertical - first Wednesday in April, we could eat afterwards."

"Of course I'll come," she covered his hand, still on her arm, squeezed ever so slightly. "Thank you, Ollie."

Chapter Nine

Another Day

Friday, on the slow train from Chelmsford, seats easier to secure, Charlotte's thoughts were deep but disjointed. She was on her way to work, where she now wanted to be - intellectual stimulus of a sort from the cases, congenial colleagues, Maddie's up-front and vulgar bluntness, Chip and Mount's quirky contrasts, above all Ollie's brainy bravado. The office was alive with the sound of more than mere existence. Even Marian and the Hard-on added to the daily doings and sexy-Sarah certainly ensured that the physical side of life could hardly ever be completely forgotten. As if Ollie, never mind Maddie, really ever would, she thought happily.

Home, however, was hardly exciting. Simon tolerated her ostentatiously. She tolerated him ostensibly. Keep apart in thought, word and deed appeared to her to have become the marital motto. As for the twins, she loved her little boys - Dan the man and Ben her baby - but they would behave like little boys and talk like little boys. With them, it seemed to her musing on the train, she missed the essential childishness of adult conversation - but was this a profound or a foolish thought? she wondered. Before deciding to return to work she felt she had had more than enough of being their full-time carer. She had

Chapter Nine

been unreservedly glad to have nanny Rosa take over, but now often felt she had been over-taken - to whom did the boys now belong? That Rosa herself undoubtedly now belonged was Charlotte's next thought, not only in the house but in the lives of the twins as well perhaps as both their parents.

After little more than a month she had realised that her life had split between office and home - manic and depressive - and might be in need of urgent treatment. What it got that particular day was a Maddie chortle as Charlotte entered the 'Council Chamber'.

"Listen to this, another satisfied customer!" she shouted and then read out:

"Dear Professor Goodman,
   You are very predictable. Your reply simply proves what I knew all along. That is, that to get a fair decision from your organisation would be as likely as being able to shove a pound of butter up a hedgehog's arse with a red hot knitting needle."

"Wow," said Charlotte. "Do we get many of those?"
"Oh sure, most of the punters get turned down as you know, and some of them can get extremely angry about it. Understandable usually - its our real service for BIG's boys: we get the nutters' abuse instead of them!"
"What about the punters who win?"
"Thank you letters, gifts sometimes, especially alcoholic ones - the Prof insists on sending all those to

the Childrens' Hospital, thinks drunken nurses a good idea - he walks home along Great Ormond Street looking out for any in need of his assistance, says it's like Gladstone's bags. Anyway he prefers rude letters, don't you Prof?" said Maddie.

Ollie had arrived for the first coffee of the morning.

"Much more interesting," he said. "A literary challenge for the writers, communicating their distress and disgust. You must come up and see my collection of the better efforts some time."

A change from etchings, Charlotte noticed, but not of principle or, she supposed, practice.

*Ninth noteworthy file -
the Case of Catch 17*

Her first file that day was one of Mount's life insurance claims, so she sought that large lady's explanations, thinking that the better safe than sorry course.

"Oh! This seemed pretty straightforward to me," said Mount. "Poor old boy died, as they do you know. Kidneys failed. Widow claimed - largish sum, for her. But hubby'd been on dialysis when he proposed just over five years ago and he'd ticked the 'no' answer to the medical question. So BIG declined the policy for non-disclosure, I agreed and so did the Prof - can't let people get away with that sort of thing, however upset the widow!"

"Why've you passed it on to me then?" Charlotte asked, puzzled.

CHAPTER NINE

Huh!" Mount snorted. "BIG spoilt it all by pulling another trick. The sum insured was £100,000 for an annual premium which BIG couldn't increase. Looked fine on the face of it, the catch was Clause 17 which allowed BIG to reduce the sum insured after five years if their actuary advised that the fixed premium was only enough for some smaller sum."

"In reality," Mount continued. "It was a type of term insurance - good for five years then start again. So what happened was that, on Fingers' advice, acting as actuary, the life cover had become a token £175 instead of £100,000. He had the nerve to suggest paying that *ex gratia* but old Mrs Carnwath rejected it - rightly - as insulting. And then the Prof got hold of the file and smelt a legal aspect. Didn't think we should accept Clause 17 as effective without considering it properly - we'll get other cases without non-disclosure to fall back on and we shouldn't set a precedent unless we're sure. He said he thought there'd been a relevant judgment recently and you'd know it."

"Ah ha, *Interfoto*!" exclaimed Charlotte.

"Abracadabra, to you too, bloody lawyers," Mount beamed benignly and moved massively away.

Charlotte found the decision at the Institute of Advanced Legal Studies in Russell Square.[12]

A Mr Beeching of Stiletto Ltd had borrowed 47 transparencies packed in a jiffy bag from a library. He did not read the delivery note, returned the transparencies a fortnight later than stipulated and was outraged to get a bill for £235 plus VAT for each day's

---

12. A court of Appeal case reported as *Inferfoto Picture Library Ltd v Stiletto Visual Programmes Ltd* [1988] 1 All England Law Reports 348.

delay totalling £3,783.50. This was strictly in accordance with one of the conditions on the back of the delivery note ('see over' was all it said on the front). However, in the Court of Appeal it failed a newly invented 'attention' test:

"If one condition in a set of printed conditions is particularly onerous or unusual, the party seeking to enforce it must show that that particular condition was fairly brought to the attention of the other party."

Charlotte realised straight away that this must be a truly devastating test for insurance policies - few would survive with their 'small print' intact. Industry lobbying had excluded them from the Unfair Contract Terms Act 1977, so they were not subject to any 'reasonableness' requirement, but this new test might prove even better as the ultimate deterrent to tricky clauses.

So she drafted a provisional decision letter to Mrs Carnwath with the good news that BIG could not rely on Clause 17, their liability would still be £100,000, but regrettably the bad news that BIG could still repudiate the policy for non-disclosure. Ollie happily approved her draft without amendment.

Then, unlocking a desk draw, he produced with a flourish his precious collection of rude letters from disappointed punters.

"Listen to these," he said, "specially selected, all addressed to me, are you sitting comfortably?"

She was, so he began to read, histrionically:

"Quite frankly your reply is no more than I

Chapter Nine

> expected as you seem to miss the point completely. If I do not get satisfaction over this matter I intend sending photocopies to *That's Life* programme on BBC1 and to the Holiday programme on BBC2 to get another opinion as to who is right."

"These are only extracts, of course," said Ollie, "I'm putting them all together for an article in the '*Post*' - to refute the insurance industry view that we're always 'consumers' champions'. Never been criticised on TV - yet!"

> "I received your decision and as prison medical reports can show I was so upset that I had a minor heart attack."

"Inside for insurance fraud!" Ollie observed. "Now for some true pomposity."
You'd recognise it, as a true practitioner of the art, thought Charlotte, but you might laugh at yourself too.

> "You must understand that to pose as independent and act in this biased manner is not only immoral but probably fraudulent and cannot continue."
>
> "I accuse your office of deceit, corruption, deception, dishonesty and hypocrisy, and challenge you to sue me so that I can bring my evidence before real arbitrators and real judges, not trumped up autocrats."

"Not a familiar expression in card-playing circles, but not necessarily inapt," Ollie said dryly.

"Unfortunately, there is no Ombudsman for complaining about Ombudsmen, so I will have to content myself with contacting the Minister and shadow Ministers responsible for Consumer Affairs."

"Who guards the guards? They can always go to court if they don't like our decisions, but that costs money - and they don't like lawyers anyway. Listen to this!"

With no other option offered, Charlotte listened.

"You have confirmed all that I have ever detested about the British Legal system. If you cannot win fairly you play 'clever clogs' with ordinary people's lives by re-writing the rules and shifting the goalposts after the game has started."

"This next is refreshingly original - one of my favourite insults." The Ombudsman seemed pleased with himself.

"This latest piece of (please supply your own epithet) has seriously and adversely affected my attitude to the entire Ombudsman apparatus. Like finding frog spawn in an otherwise entirely irreproachable container of guaranteed pure milk."

Chapter Nine

"But this last one is definitely not a favourite. Read it for yourself." Ollie held out a letter with large green hand-writing.

Charlotte read it

> "Now explain fuck brain the logic/fairness in this. Then arsehole then call yourself an Ombudsman. Frustrating it is when fuck heads like you rob the air of breath from the others around. What a waste of fucking life you are.
>
> Yours a policyholder.
> PS PHYSICAL I COULD GET VIOLENT."

"We reported him to the police - he'd thoughtfully written his name and address on the envelope. A friendly neighbourhood bobby called on him and the door was answered by an OAP wearing slippers and a cardy and walking with a Zimmer frame! He promised to behave himself in future," Ollie obviously found it funny.

Charlotte thought it sad. She asked: "Do losers never write nice letters?"

"A few," he replied, "but not often quotably. Although there was one lady who called me a watchdog unwilling to bite the hand that fed me - 'the occasional nip would be alright as long as it did not draw blood' - and then sent me a Christmas card picturing a dove carrying an olive branch. She'd written inside 'you're only doing your job, I know that.'"

"Well I'd better go and do my job. And if anything

rude comes in, be sure you'll get it!" said Charlotte standing up.

As she left the room, Ollie said: "I'll get Mrs Arden to do the Carnwath letter, see if it provokes anything interesting."

Many a true word, she thought - later. At the time she only thought: what does he want now? as she saw Marian the Manager in wait for her at his door.

"A word," he leered, moustache twitching. She thought of a word but went in without saying it.

"In my capacity as Clerk to Council, I have to inform you that there will be a Meeting of Council on Wednesday the fourth of April and you are required to make yourself available."

"What on earth for?" she asked.

"I expect they all want to see why the Ombudsman seems so happy with office life these days! Or then again it might be to do with Mr Scott's agenda item about excessively legalistic decisions. The Prof will be there too so you can discuss it with him in advance - whichever it is - at Stefano's *ce soir* perhaps."

"It's Italian, not French," she said. "When and where is the Meeting?"

"You will be duly notified in writing in due course, but it's 11am at the Russell. By the way, you might also like to discuss with the Prof who this Ann is who keeps ringing him up - and where they're going for the weekend!"

So that's what he wanted, she thought as she left, hiding her huff and also thinking: but I'd better find out - bloody sods, both of them.

CHAPTER NINE

Tenth file - The Case of the Brave Balcony Hopper

Returning to the Council Room she shared with Maddie, Charlotte was irritated to find it empty. She needed a therapeutic grumble. Instead she opened another file. Are they all to be tragic? she wondered.

Evans-Lombe junior, Eddie to his mates, had died after falling from the third floor balcony of a holiday hotel. Apparently stepping fearlessly from one balcony across a narrow gap to the next balcony was the customary way in which youthful guests visited other rooms - quicker, and discreter, than the corridor. Happily, for his grieving father seeking pecuniary consolation, Eddie had bought a BIG travel policy, sold automatically as an 'add-on' to the holiday - profitable for the travel agent because of the substantial commission percentage and even for BIG, but only if no claims had to be paid. This policy, as advertised in the holiday brochure, included a death benefit of £15,000. Unhappily, for Eddie's greedy father, the policy small print of the policy, unlike the large print of the advert, expressly excluded claims arising from:

> "Winter sports, motor cycling, mountaineering, pot-holing, riding or driving in any kind of race, underwater activities or any other wilful exposure to risk."

To father's furious disappointment, forthrightly communicated, Arms had relied on the last six words of this exclusion clause as letting BIG off. Maddie had agreed with Arms. He was not surprised since he too could clearly recall another case of hers where a teenager had daringly participated in a local tourist attraction of diving from a very high bridge with, for him, a fatal result. Although common among tourists - diving, not dying - the Prof had found the photographs of the bridge frightening and accepted BIG's exclusion of liability.

However, in Eddie's case, the Prof had had second thoughts. Whilst the diving had appeared to him to have been the same sort of pre-arranged dangerous activity as the others specified in the exclusion clause, balcony-hopping looked different - and not just because the photographs were less frightening. Stepping from one balcony to another could be in the same class as road-crossing - wilful and risky, especially abroad, yet surely any accidental deaths should fall, as it were, fairly and reasonably within the policy. The file carried a sticker on which Maddie had scribbled 'LLL' - 'Let Lottie Look'. Those initials could become unwelcome, thought Charlotte.

Nevertheless, she did pretend to do some research at the Institute of Advanced Legal Studies, always an acceptable excuse for escaping from the office. To her surprise, she actually discovered a Scottish decision in 1896 giving a helpful judicial test.[13] In that court case, the policyholder, a foolhardy Englishman, had drowned when bathing alone from a boat in a Highland loch one freezing April evening: he had failed to appreciate the awful effect of cold water. Despite a similar exclusion

---

13. Reported as *Sangster v General Accident* (1896) 24 R(Ct of Sess) 56.

CHAPTER NINE

clause, his insurer was made to pay up. The test of 'wilful exposure to risk', said the court, is subjective: did the deceased himself - not others older and wiser - think he was doing something dangerous? Applying this test to dead Eddie, the fatally unfortunate balcony hopper, Charlotte was satisfied that BIG should pay up too - even though it would not be to a needy Scottish widow. Ollie readily agreed with her. So Evans-Lombe senior lost a son but won £15,000.

That evening at Stefano's, Charlotte reported that Arms had been very angry: he regarded the payment as an undeserved profit for the father and an encouragement to irresponsible behaviour on the part of Eddie-like policyholders.

Ollie shrugged: "He's a general insurer and exactly that can be said of life insurance itself."

Then, as he drank, she asked, to see if he would splutter: "What are you up to with Ann this weekend?"

Not a spot of splutter, she noted and thought: but he spills very little wine.

"Bridge," he replied. "Worthing, we play there with a party of friends from the Monday Club - so-called because it meets on Tuesdays! There is an explanation but you don't want to hear it. Ann Hughes from the Law Commission, I told you about her. Nothing else going on if that's what you're worried about. What made you ask?"

"Oh, just something someone said at the office," she said, thinking: this calls for double-checking just in case of double-crossing.

Later, at home, she rang Timmy Lloyd.

"Do me a favour for old times' sake?" she asked eventually.

"Anyfin' dahlin', within reason natch."

"Well, a little bird tells me you'll be spending the weekend in Worthing."

"Wha' lil' bird?"

"Let's just say a tartan variety," she said carefully, noting the absence of any denial.

"Scottie you mean, Mr Scott to you I spec', what of it?"

"It won't be possible for me to get to Worthing myself, family commitments," she lied, realising it was unconvincing, "So I wondered if you'd feel able to let me know the gist of your report as well, so that I can be prepared for developments, you understand."

He laughed: "Course I unnerstan', dahlin', you wan' me to keep me weather eye on your Ombudsmanny for personal reasons, blow the gaff if he gets up to no good, off on his tod like, without his latest bit of skirt!"

God almighty, she thought, why does an Oxford graduate have to affect such an awful accent - and slang from nowhere - maybe it impresses clients, think they're dealing with a denizen of the underworld; Arms the actuary may even imagine he's met the real world. But what can Timmy possibly know about Ollie and me - there's nothing to know, yet. All she said was:

"Off the record, of course."

"Natch, dahlin'."

Chapter Ten

Gloomy Monday

Weekends led Charlotte to gloomy Monday mornings - too much spouse, not enough twins, nanny in the ointment and in-laws in everything, all hung over, often into the afternoon. Easter had been horribly unendurable whilst ordinary weekends were merely awful. Maddie, having learnt this, would attempt to lighten the week's beginning. So she often tried to amuse her roommate on arrival by offering a tit-bit from her own cases. But they did tend towards blacker humour.

To-day's welcomer was poor Peter Millett. On holiday in Spain with his missus, watching a fiesta celebrating the Armada's great victory when a ball from a loose cannon blew off his right foot. BIG's travel policy covers: "total loss by physical severance of one or both feet - £25,000." Happily or unhappily, however, thanks to his wife catching the foot and a miracle of micro-surgery, it was re-attached.

Making a drama out of a trauma, Arms had refused to pay for Peter's foot:

"It's not lost, he's wearing it."

Charlotte delivered her fully considered legal opinion rather shortly but in language a laywomen, especially one like Maddie, could understand:

"Bollocks!"

Then their shared phone rang. Maddie answered, passed it over:

"For you, a Mr Timothy, Sarah says, personal," and mouthed: "she'll be listening."

Charlotte said: "Ms Angus speaking."

"Lloyd Timothy here," an impeccable Oxford accent, "concerning your holiday enquiry."

Very subtle, she thought, saying: "Oh yes."

"Nothing to report, I'm afraid, at least not yet. Our friend tried out one of the back single rooms over the weekend, no disturbances at all. Against that his travelling companion hardly slept a wink, double room with sea view, other people coming - and going - throughout the night."

She felt more relieved than she had expected.

"Thank you, Mr Timothy," she said, adding but not wholly meaning, "I'm very grateful. Better luck next time perhaps."

"My client will certainly hope so."

"Who was that then, who're you having it off with, you old slag?" Maddie enquired, with her customary delicacy.

"Never you mind," said Charlotte, "Not one of yours, anyway, wouldn't touch any of them with a barge-pole."

"It's that dick, isn't it, Timmy Lloyd?"

"Shut your face."

"Now, now, ladies, I've come for coffee and civilised conversation," Ollie intervened, arriving as always without warning.

"You can shut your face too," was Maddie's uncivilised response, whereas Charlotte asked more relevantly:

Chapter Ten

"How was the bridge?"

"Terrible," he replied. "We began not badly - Friday evening I won the funny hat prize for winning a trick with the two of clubs."

Complete incomprehension greeted this information.

"Anyway we finished in the first five. After that Ann's concentration went, tired quickly."

Fits Timmy's tale, thought Charlotte.

"By Sunday the lols were at our throats."

"What the Hell are lols?" screeched Maddie.

"Little old ladies," Ollie explained. "Do-gooder Judges like Denning always think they need protection from wicked young men such as me."

Young, thought Charlotte, he's feeling frisky to-day, must have slept well.

"But bridge players know better - give 'em half a chance and the lols'll take you to pieces, mercilessly. Pity Denning didn't play bridge, no 'new equity' to plague law students, lols can look out for themselves! On the other hand in chess it's the rat-faced juniors who'll delight in savaging an elderly gentleman like me."

Gentleman, thought Charlotte, whatever next? She at least, having read law, understood most of his wittering.

The Ombudsman left his young ladies, cup in hand, frowning at memories, to their own devices.

Eleventh file - the Joy-Rider Case

Charlotte's chosen device was to return to work. She picked up and perused the next file on her pile. It was one of Chip's, to do with a car: joy-riding. She went for a tactful consultation with that little Liverpudlian.

"The commonest case," Chip explained, fag in hand instead of draw, "is the policyholder's son finding his father's keys and taking a few friends for a drive - almost inevitably, at least that's all we see, the car's written-off. If Dad's policy was comprehensive, the damage would be covered. But if it was only 'third party, fire and theft', no cover - theft requires in law an intent to deprive permanently, and unless sonny boy was running away from home this requirement would not be satisfied. Different if the joy-rider was a stranger, but BIG disliked this too. So they have a standard endorsement. Here read this."

Chip picked a copy of BIG's motor policy from her desk and pointed to a paragraph on the back. Charlotte as instructed read it:

"The company shall be under no liability in connection with any insured vehicle whilst such vehicle is being driven or used by any person other than the policyholder."

"In other words," Chip went on, "punter-drivers are not covered for joy-riders." Charlotte left the fag-fumed room thankfully, wondering what the problem would be with the case and why the 'no-smoking' policy could not be enforced.

Chapter Ten

Reading the file further, however, she soon found the problem: Steven Sedley's Jag had been joy-ridden but not damaged - it was apparently parked and left in one piece and then stolen. His sorry stepson's story - "it was alright when we left it but gone when we came out of the club" - was swallowed whole. But Arms, on BIG's behalf, still declined payment for the theft in reliance on the endorsement. Chip, although sympathising with step-father Steven - about the loss of his wheels as well - tended to agree with Arm's but Charlotte, predictably by now, disagreed. When the car was actually stolen it was not being driven or used by anyone, except of course the thief herself - stepson's current 'squeeze' was chief suspect. So the endorsement could not be relied upon. Ollie, equally predictably, agreed with Charlotte's strict construction against BIG, the drafters of policy, which meant that the endorsement simply did not apply and they would have to pay up. Arms as always was extremely angry - indeed he became threatening on the phone:

"I'll get the dirt on the bastard sooner or later, then he'll see sense - or else," he had shouted at Charlotte.

She thought she knew what he meant.

"What do you think of this," cried Maddie, volume as always up. "Granny Gibson's fridge-freezer broke down, spoiling all her lovely meat. She'd bought one of BIG's frozen food policies and her granddaughter put in a claim for a list of joints and cuts weighing in total 93lbs - she said this was simply one week's meals for a senior citizen and potential visitors. But I've got the same model, the cubic capacity of the freezer compartment is 42lbs maximum. Greedy eh? Prof wouldn't give her anything - didn't come with clean hands - but I blame the granddaughter. Vegetarianism must be the best policy!"

"Let's grab a quick bite," said Charlotte, "before the rush. Granny's made me feel peckish, but I don't want a drink."

"You think you're spending enough time in wine bars with the Prof," jeered Maddie. "You'll be turning into an alcoholic - I know what he's like."

"No, no," Charlotte protested. "I really am a teetotaller, but only in moderation, of course."

"Yeah, only between drinks."

They smiled and waved at Sarah, mouthing 'back soon', as they left. She was on the phone. Ollie's door was closed - more bridge, he had said, groaning happily.

Sitting outside at the table outside a superior sandwich-bar in Sicilian Avenue, convenient but still too chilly, warmed by soup and a hot bacon baguette each, plus a couple of cappuccinos, eventually Maddie asked:

"Does the Prof know about Timmy?"

"No but I'm certainly going to tell him and it's not what you think, just his professional relationship with BIG."

"Well don't get caught by their family policy."

"What do you mean?"

"Oh just an insurance industry joke, trotted out regularly in after-dinner speeches," Maddie explained. "It's about sexual relationships - Legal & General means marriage, Co-operative Insurance is cohabitation,

Chapter Ten

Commercial Union prostitution, Sun Alliance means a holiday romance, General Accident a one-night stand, Domestic & General adultery, Professional Life - you and the Prof!"

Charlotte threw her scrunched-up serviette at Maddie who carried on:

"And there are a few rude versions involving Equine & Livestock and NFU Mutual - national farmers union - whilst BIG is, of course, pregnancy."

"No fear of that," snorted Charlotte, thinking not while I take the pill and hoping Maddie would think she meant that intercourse was out of the question.

"Would Arms play dirty tricks on us?" she asked.

"He has tried," Maddie replied. "Somehow he learnt about my little fling with the Prof, I think Marian told him, and he warned me if we got it wrong on one particular case he'd tell the world. By then I didn't care and the Prof didn't know so we went ahead anyway. Nothing happened."

"Why not?" Charlotte had an idea.

"He never said anything, but I don't imagine Arms had an attack of conscience - he's always convinced he's right and really believes he has a sacred duty to defend BIG against bad claims. No I think he simply hadn't got any hard evidence."

"I see," said Charlotte, wondering if she cared and if Ollie would care. "Let's go back."

Sarah was still on the phone but she smiled and waved at them whilst continuing her conversation - apparently frightfully funny things had happened at the weekend. As they entered, Ollie's door opened, three strangers emerged and Mrs Arden marched them out of the office. One of them was female.

So that's his bridge partner, thought Charlotte, nice bit of plump, but bags under her eyes, short of sleep perhaps. She wondered whether frightfully funny things had happened to her too at the weekend.

Twelfth file - the Case of the Drugged Deceased

Following Maddie back into their room, Charlotte somewhat unenthusiastically picked up the next file, anticipating another sad story. She was not disappointed even though Rock-star 'wannabe' Paul Kennedy had died happy - very happy - on his way to a 'gig' in Dublin.

Paul's wife Felicity had far-sightedly insured his life with BIG just before he travelled - large sum for large premium:

"I always knew he was not long for this world, the good die young, and I had to look after meself, don't you know," she had explained.

Fingers lacked Arms's nose, as to sensitivity not size, but even he smelt something fishy and he refused payment. The trouble was that Paul had not been good at all. The cause of his death was an over-dose of the controlled drugs he had been attempting to smuggle into Ireland - in his bowels, the condom had burst. It was the drugs not the condom that the Irish found offensive.

Refusal to pay up on the life assurance taken out by Felicity was based on various grounds. First, the policy

CHAPTER TEN

contained an exclusion of liability where the deceased died "at his own hand." Assuming that Paul had stuffed himself unaided, so to speak, literally this exclusion might apply. However Mount was vehement that it contemplated suicide, deliberate death not accidental. No-one dared disagree.

Secondly, Fingers pointed out that admission of a death claim was expressly "dependent upon production of evidence satisfactory to the directors" whereas here he personally could confirm that the directors were definitely dissatisfied. Again Mount knew what this provision was supposed to mean and that was evidence of the death itself - it was directed against missing presumed dead claims, or 'Lucans' as they were known in the industry. No dissent stood a chance with her: Paul's death was amply evidenced, not simply by a doctor's certificate, but by terrified testimony from other passengers on the Ryanair flight on which he performed his final frenzied 'gig'.

Thirdly, looking outside the policy, Fingers asserted that Felicity's claim was unenforceable at common law because she had to rely on illegalities to sustain it. This was the point at which reference was made to Charlotte as technical or "too difficult". She, however, felt no difficulty in rejecting the assertion: the policy covered death irrespective of cause, save for excluding suicide. Felicity only needed to establish that Paul had died without relying on why.

Fourthly and finally, Fingers submitted that it would be contrary to public policy to let Felicity profit from insuring the life of a criminal committing crimes - the flood-gates would be opened to bank robbers' molls and terrorists' dolls, crime would be encouraged as a career for the caring! Despite having some sympathy for the submission, Charlotte did not accept it in the circumstances of the case: the weakness was the lack of any evidence, as opposed to suspicion, that Felicity had been aware of Paul's activities, much less condoned them.

So BIG was required to pay the claim, with interest. Fingers' displeasure was palpable but to his credit he paid up even though the amount exceeded the scheme's £100,000 limit. Charlotte thought that secretly he felt a little sorry for Felicity - a gentle girl fallen amongst yobs and left bereaved and destitute.

Susceptible softy, she also thought.

"I'm conducting a poll," called out Chip, as she 'borrowed' a cup of coffee. "Is a ceramic hob 'glass'?"

"You mean within breakage cover?" Maddie asked. "Course it is - benefit of doubt to policyholder, eh Lot?"

She nodded.

"OK that's a majority, 3 to 1, Mount against, but she thought a woman stupid enough to drop a casserole from high enough to crack her hob didn't deserve to win."

"Alright, my turn," Maddie shouted, "also cracked glass. My punter's hobby was exotic fish - keeping not eating - he lost £500 worth when his aquarium leaked until it was empty. But BIG's contents policy excludes 'livestock or pets.' He says his fish are neither, they're just the raw material of his hobby, and should be covered by the policy as 'household goods or personal effects'.

Chapter Ten

"Were any of them called Wanda?" asked Chip.

"And did they get eaten and if so fried or raw?" added Charlotte.

"Shut your faces," argued Maddie. "I thought they were still pets, despite the hobby, outside the policy - and so did the Prof. But BIG had to replace the aquarium itself - broken glass!"

Later at Stefano's, Charlotte said:

"Council Meeting next Wednesday, I've been summoned, to face charges of being a lawyer. Should I plead guilty?"

"Doesn't matter, there's no penalty," Ollie replied. "It's only a talking-shop. Never makes any decisions - BIG's Bob does that and tells Cocksey who tells Council what they've decided. They're always moaning about the 'tone and terminology' of decision letters and the 'principles and precedents' involved - they're not supposed to discuss individual decisions just because they don't like them, but that's what they're really doing."

He shrugged, hands apart and palms up: "But it's all to no purpose - I refer to papers they've not seen and law cases they've never heard of, infuriates them. Cocksey won't have understood what anyone's been talking about anyway and Bob won't have told her what to decide so she'll cut discussion off in mid-flow, saying 'we must move on to the next business - the Ombudsman is aware of Council''s views and will take account of them in future'. I nod. Then the office boy garbles the matter for the minutes - not deliberately, he'll have missed the point - and corrections won't be tolerated by Cocksey at the next meeting. So that's the end of the matter - they can forget about it and have a jolly good lunch."

"Is it jolly? Don't the others on Council object to being treated like that?" asked Charlotte.

"Wouldn't bring them any joy, she models herself on Mrs T - you've seen the handbag, an offensive weapon *per se* in her hands. But you're right, they don't like it. I've often enough over-heard her called 'Attilla the Hen'! She's up for re-election on Wednesday, but don't bet on an upset."

"What about the wine-tasting, are we still on for that?" asked Charlotte.

"Absolutely, although after Council Meetings my drinking need is not so much quality as quantity. Should be interesting, the proprietor will be speaking, he's French of course, and there'll be a party of American lawyers, over here for some Conference. Hope you won't have to hurry off. . . Lot?"

"So do I," she said. "But there's something you should know."

When Ollie had heard her suspicions about Arms and Timmy Lloyd, he thought for a while before saying:

"Well we'll just have make sure he sees nothing worth reporting."

"So I should go home early?" she said, disappointedly she thought.

"No, no, no, we'll give him the slip!" he said, excitedly she thought.

Chapter Eleven

Nearly Wednesday

Tuesday morning, the train to Liverpool Street stood stationary but not at a station. Signal-failure had been blamed but the commuters merely muttered. Charlotte sat looking through the carriage's grimy window but without seeing the gardens and yards backing onto the railway. She was replaying last night's lying, not with but to Simon. He had been told, with a groan, of the Council Meeting to which she had been summoned. True that far but about to be elaborated. It would take place in the evening, at the Russell, followed by a buffet meal with drinks to which she had been invited, along with the other three Assistants and, of course, the Ombudsman and the Office Manager and even the awesome Mrs Arden and the lovely Sarah. BIG's Bob was expected too. All to mark the second anniversary of the founding of the Scheme, she had explained at, she now felt, incriminating length.

No spouses, partners or cohabs, for fear of whom Sarah, not to mention Robin or perhaps the Ombudsman, would bring, she had heard herself insinuating. And since this extraordinary function, to which duty called her, might terminate late, Maddie had kindly suggested that she stay with her over-night at the Barbican flat funded by her current grey gentleman. Somewhat to her surprise, Simon had seemed to swallow this story satisfactorily. No questions from him to test her lies, or indeed at all. However, Maddie's corroboration of the alibi was still to be sought. Doubtless forthcoming, she thought, but not without rude and ribald comment.

Later than usual at the office, Charlotte's arrival met Maddie's cry:

"Was your train deranged, then?"

"Derailed?"

"No, was it subject to derangement?"

"I felt deranged by the delay," Charlotte said. "But what on earth are you getting at? Try to talk sense for a change - I'm not one of your dirty old men!"

The explanation for Maddie's peculiar question was the wording to be found in BIG's travel policies. These incorporated a standard insurance industry provision, derived from a long forgotten source, which covered by payment of a modest sum - £40 - the peril of holiday departure being delayed for more than eleven hours because of any of a number of specified causes. One of these causes was "derangement" of an aircraft. Arms insisted that this meant that the plane itself must have been deranged by suffering some mechanical breakdown or structural defect. BIG did not, he said forcefully, intend to cover delays due to derangement at air-traffic control, such as computer crashes or, acutely, the 'work-to-rule' during 1988 of Spanish air-traffic controllers. One £40 might be neither here nor there but thousands of £40s becomes an issue of principle.

From her brokering background, Maddie knew that

Chapter Eleven

such a high percentage commission was paid to travel agents that travel policies became completely unprofitable for insurers if any claims at all were paid. She also knew how they were sold: 'no worries, happy holidays, everything covered!' Actually delays due to 'industrial action' were within the policy but arguably, according to our own Civil Aviation Authority, the Spanish delay had been a work-to-rule in the interests of passenger safety. Nevertheless, in Maddie's opinion, expressed to Arms with equal force, the claims should be treated as coming well within the spirit of travel insurance.

As to the letter, she had consulted the Oxford English Dictionary which told her, not helpfully, that "derangement" meant: "The act of deranging, or fact of being deranged; disorder; confusion; insanity." The verb "derange" itself enjoyed an unusually unhelpful definition beginning: "Not in Johnson who considered the word to be French." The reference was to the dead Doctor's dictionary, but the living Ombudsman had consulted his wife who had not disagreed. So, in the light of the linguistic position, not to mention Maddie's forceful guidance as to what would be 'fair and reasonable', Ollie had decided to make BIG pay all the £40s. Maddie was crowing with triumph, although Arms had apparently growled ominously something about deranging the scheme and everyone in it.

My train was no less deranged than everybody else, thought Charlotte, carrying a mug of coffee over to her end of the table where her files had been piled.

Thirteenth and Final File - a Funeral Expenses Case

Death is never far from insurance, was the depressed and, perhaps, profound pensée striking Charlotte as she read her bottom - so far - file.

A BIG mailshot had hit a pensioner, old Martin Nourse. Aimed at enabling the avoidance of financial if not emotional embarrassment for family and friends, as well as of posthumous personal humiliation, following inevitable if not necessarily imminent decease, a modest monthly amount would provide for a decent and dignified funeral and perhaps a party. More precisely, the brochure's table showed that, for a 66-year old male, just under £9 per month would secure a death benefit of just over £1,000. Could poor old Martin have been expected to realise that, with his own healthy life expectancy, the time could very likely come when he would actually have paid more than that promised benefit?

Perhaps he might have realised. But from the glossy literature that fell through his letterbox it had actually been too difficult for dear old Martin to appreciate that the cover would have cost him more than the £1,000 benefit, not after the 10 years approximately of a fairly elementary calculation, but in fact in 6 years or so when compound interest lost was taken into account. Nor had he appreciated that there would then be a near-negligible surrender value and that to preserve the death benefit, decreasing in value because of inflation, good money would have to be thrown after bad for the

CHAPTER ELEVEN

rest of his life. Nor had sad old Martin grasped the somewhat significant point that, on his death within the first 2 years, instead of the £1,000, all that would be available for funeral and party would be repayment of premiums, plus 10%. The direct mail manner of marketing the policy meant that there had been no intermediary involved to explain its provisions to stupid old Martin and to offer advice as to any alternatives.

Despite the passage of several years, Charlotte concluded that the policy should be set aside and lucky old Martin put into the position he would have been in had he saved instead with a respectable Building Society. She hoped no-one would suggest that that was a contradiction in terms, as she knew people did sometimes with the expression, often used in leases, 'reputable insurer'. Ollie readily agreed with her conclusion. His basis in principle was that sellers of insurance, especially long-term, should ensure that each potential policyholder understands what he is buying, both the minuses and the pluses. In practice, she thought, the probable basis for his agreement had been a calculation as to the comparative quantity and quality of wine becoming affordable for dead old Martin's wake - coupled with a vain hope that a funeral expenses Ombudsman might be invited.

Fingers was furious: a nice little earner turned into a loss leader. If nasty old Martin were to broadcast his outrageous fortune, BIG would be inundated with wrinkly punters wanting their money back despite having been covered for donkey's years. The shareholders' dividend would be disappointing. The

Board would be displeased. He would only pay on condition that old Martin kept it confidential.

"You can try it on if you like," said Ollie, as if judiciously. "But I'm not prepared to impose any such unwarranted and unenforceable restriction."

Adding insult to injury, as so often, thought Charlotte.

All Fingers said, however, was: "The future of the scheme will have to be reassessed seriously this time - you may have gone too far for your own good!"

As he left, Ollie called after him: "See you after lunch, Mr Lightman."

"What's happening after lunch?" asked Charlotte.

"An oral hearing, one of the few, Mount's case, she'll be prosecutor, I'll be judge, you'd better come as court clerk - Maddie's bagged bailiff, though she doesn't know what it means. Anyway you might as well come and listen, could be interesting of course, but it'll happen in your Council Chamber so you'd have to squat somewhere else if you wanted to do any work."

"Why not hold the hearing in your room?"

"Too small, there'll be Mr and Mrs Parker - the punters - Fingers and his salesman, plus four of us. But there's actually a much better reason: when hearings have ended, at least as far as I'm concerned, the parties often don't want to leave and go on arguing or shouting at each other as well as at me, so I like to be able to walk out and leave them to it - used to chair Rent Tribunals where tempers were often lost and a retiring room was essential, mind you there were three of us to go and the last one out could get caught anyway if we

Chapter Eleven

weren't quick enough."

"So the Tribunal clerks had to separate the parties?"

"Exactly."

"Oh thank you very much," said Charlotte, thinking of Maddie, or better Mount, doubling as a bouncer. "What's the hearing about?"

"Misselling of a personal pension."

"OK, I'll play clerk to your Lord Denning - a judge who thought he was an Ombudsman, I once heard an after-dinner speaker say - but what about the Board, will they consider winding-up the scheme?"

"Not to worry," gestured Ollie, adding delphically: "Fingers' poke packs no pig, won't catch the eye of BIG's Bob."

He didn't explain this obscurity but continued: "Anyway the Board members all have different agendas, depending on their own personal aspirations. Have you heard the one about running an insurance company being like driving a car, but the Managing Director will have his hands on the steering wheel, the Advertising Manager's foot will be on the accelerator, the Finance Director's on the brake, whilst the Auditor navigates by looking out of the rear window."

"Another after-dinner special?" queried Charlotte. "Not too subtle for insurance men?"

"Not filthy you mean," said Ollie - she had - "but lawyers and especially accountants find it amusing."

An after-drinks joke, she concluded, only a very well-oiled audience could actually laugh at it.

That afternoon, at a quarter past two precisely, Maddie as over-acting court official ushered the

Ombudsman, clothed-all in charcoal-grey, together with Charlotte his clerk into the Council Chamber to perform their quasi-judicial roles. The parties were already present, seated either side of the table, with prosecutor Mount sitting grimly at the far end. The Parkers started to stand as Ollie entered only to be waved down. Fingers remained stoically sitting, but his salesman jumped up. It was the rep Charlotte had spotted outside court, at the centre of *Saunders v BIG*, the endowment mortgage scam case.

Shorter than Ollie, red-face, handle-bar moustache, balding, brightly-coloured bow-tie, he was dressed like a bookie in a loud check suit. Charlotte saw that he was wearing thick gold rings and a bracelet. The distinguishing marks of the life insurance salesman, worn to demonstrate personal prosperity to prospective punters, Charlotte thought, honey for the bees or was he a fly-catcher?

Waving-down failed. The salesman advanced on Ollie enthusiastically, then caught and shook his waving hand vigorously.

"Hi! Micky Hart from BIG - here's my card. Saw you in court in the Tommy Sunders case. Didn't speak then but I'm very happy to have this opportunity of helping you to sort out this mix-up - and afterwards, if there's any financial advice you need, spare funds or investments not really working for you, let me buy you a drink somewhere and we can talk about it."

Fingers' hands had covered his face. He removed them to grip Micky sharply, and evidently painfully, by the upper-arm. Then he hissed: "Sit Hart!"

Chapter Eleven

Micky sat.

Ollie smiled weakly and turned to the other side:

"You must be Mr and Mrs Parker," he said, shaking each of them by the hand. "I'm so glad you could manage to get here - I know it was a nuisance, but a meeting like this seemed to me the best way to progress your complaint."

The Parkers, a scrawny smile-free couple in their late fifties, wore mackintoshes - they had refused to part with them. Mr Parker asked: "Wha' abaht me loss of earnin's, then?"

"You already know we can't reimburse those, only reasonable travelling expenses. However, we understood you were working evening shifts now?"

"Yeah, but it's the principle, ain' it."

Ollie turned back to Fingers, saying: "We'd better shake hands too, Mr Lightman, to complete the set."

They did so, exchanging scowls that might have been mistaken for formal smiles.

Seating himself at the head of the table, with Charlotte to his right, Ollie said:

"Let me make some introductions. As you will surely have realised, I am the Ombudsman, Professor Goodman. I believe that Mr and Mrs Parker and Mr Hart are already acquainted - indeed, that's essentially why we're all here to-day, ha ha!"

No-one else looked amused, Charlotte noticed, not even Micky Hart, and Mrs Parker whined:

"No I ain't met 'im - if I'd a bin there, we wouldn't be 'ere now."

Undaunted Ollie proceeded: "Next to Mr Hart is

Mr Lightman - BIG's finance director who wrote to you about your complaint."

Perfunctory nods transmitting hostility, Charlotte observed to herself.

"Everyone else present belongs to my office - at the end of the table is Mrs Mountford, the Technical Assistant in charge of this case; next to me is Ms Angus, a solicitor, well-qualified to assist me with any necessary legal advice."

Fingers gave Charlotte a look which she thought dirty.

"And sitting by the door is Ms Hill, another Technical Assistant here to act as a sort of umh. . ."

"Gofer," giggled Maddie.

"Quite," Ollie continued explaining. "This is not a court of law, I'm not a judge and the procedure will be as informal as possible. Mr Parker, as the complainant, you should begin by telling me what your complaint is - although I have read all the papers, there could be points you wish to emphasise - I may interrupt for the purposes of clarification and Mrs Mountford may want to bring out additional aspects. Then Mr Lightman will be allowed to ask relevant questions - to test what you've said, like a cross-examination in court but gentler, of course."

Ollie gave Fingers a look which Charlotte thought not undirty.

"After that I will expect Mr Hart to give his version of what occurred, answering questions from Mr Lightman, myself and Mrs Mountford, again in the interests of clarification, before you can cross-examine

CHAPTER ELEVEN

him in your turn. Finally, you'll have an opportunity to say whatever you feel appropriate to me, by way of having the last word."

"Wha' abaht me? It's me 'ouse-keepin' at stake," Mrs Parker whinged aggressively.

"In the circumstances, you will be allowed to assist your husband with his questions and statements," Ollie replied graciously. Her husband explained:

"She alwuss 'as the lass word."

"Well Mr Parker, if that's all clear, tell me about your complaint," said Ollie the Ombudsman in what, Charlotte assumed, he thought was an informal, user-friendly way.

"It's all in me letters, they messed me abaht sumfink rotten - wants our money back, thas' all," was the not very user-friendly reply.

"Mrs Mountford, perhaps you could lead Mr Parker briefly through the salient facts given in his letters of complaint," Ollie patiently passed the buck.

So Mount led him: "You've worked for the same firm, printers and publishers, for over thirty years, joining its pension scheme from the beginning?"

"Yeah, thas right."

"Last year, after meeting Mr Hart, you agreed to transfer out of the firm's occupational pension scheme into a personal pension scheme with BIG?"

"Yeah course I did - thas why we're 'ere."

"Did you have any comparison of the benefits under the firm's scheme and under BIG's scheme?"

"Nah, don' remember any fink like tha'."

"Did Mr Martin warn you that you might be worse

Love At All Risks

off in BIG's scheme?"

"Nah, she did," Mr Parker jerked his thumb at his wife.

"Yeah, when 'e tole me wha' e'd gorn an' dun, I din 'alf give 'im a earful, but 'e din't lissen," she confirmed.

"An' then they got the bleedin' paperwork all wrong, so she 'ad me write, but that got sweet FA off of 'em!" Mr Parker was warming to his grievance.

"'E's fed-up wi' 'em - we only wants our money back," whined his wife.

"How did you come to meet Mr Hart?" asked Ollie.

"Saw one of 'em BIG adverts with little sods changing jobs, jus' arf'er 'earin' that guvverment bloke on telly bangin' on abaht 'portable pensions - break your chains' 'e said - so I 'phoned 'em up an' 'e called round," said Mr Parker.

"I was aht, at Bingo, wurss luck," scowled Mrs P.

"What made you interested in portability?"

"Firm 'ad been taken-over by the Mirror, rubbish rag, an' I din' trust that fat bastard - Maxwell, bloody foreigner, - notice went rahnd wiv 'is grinnin' gob, only goin' to take-over the bleedin' pension scheme an all, din' like the sound of it."

"Did Mr Hart offer any advice?"

"Tole me where to sign, said BIG's pension was a nice little earner and I'd not be sorry 'avin' it."

"But you're sorry already," Fingers responded to Ollie's gesture inviting questions, and attempted - unsuccessfully - the common touch. "We've had a few administration problems processing the paperwork - transfers out and opt outs have proved unexpectedly

Chapter Eleven

popular and indeed profitable - but a BIG personal pension, like a pet at Christmas, is supposed to be for life, ha ha - a long-term investment. Isn't it a little premature to want to return this particular pet for an M and S refund?"

Mr and Mrs Parker glared at each other before the latter objected: "Marks don't sell pets."

Ollie intervened: "He's asking why you changed your mind so soon about changing pensions."

"Well we got this bumf abaht benefits bein' better wiv Capn Bob in charge of pensions so she said. . ."

"I said, tole you so, should've listened to me an' stayed wiv the old firm," interjected his wife, self-righteously.

"You are aware," said Fingers, "that after you complained we enquired about transferring you back into your occupational scheme but unfortunately they wouldn't have you except at a much higher value than we received from them?"

"Thas why we jus' wants our money back," Mr Parker explained assertively.

"Mr Hart," Ollie addressed the hitherto surprisingly silent salesman. "Exactly what advice did you give to Mr Parker?"

"Well hi there again Johnny," Micky spoke directly to his punter. "I didn't have to give you any advice, did I? You'd already made up your mind, hadn't you? Decided to escape from Maxwell, out of the boss's pension and into your own, that'd show 'em all eh?"

Mr Parker nodded his head slowly, evidently in agreement; Mrs Parker shook her head quickly, evidently in disagreement. She had not been present,

Charlotte recalled, but perhaps she was one of the people being shown.

"So you see, Oliver," the salesman directed his sincerity towards the Ombudsman, who flinched. "It was what we in the industry call 'execution only', no questions, no answers, just the paperwork." He beamed at Ollie, who observed:

"And easily earned commission, then, eh?"

"Rough with the smooth, rough with the smooth!" Micky replied happily. Fingers' face, however, expressed unhappiness.

The Ombudsman smiled ominously: "Mrs Mountford, your witness."

"It is right, isn't it, Mr Hart," enquired the prosecutor, standing to tower over the accused salesman, "that Mr Parker's benefits under his firm's scheme would be significantly better in every respect than under BIG's personal pension policy?"

"Well I didn't know that at the time, dearie, what's your name, Victoria is it?"

A glowering Mount ignored his question:

"But you know it now, don't you? And you would have expected it then, wouldn't you?"

"Not every respect," protested Micky. "Our personal pensions include a guaranteed annuity rate."

"Not worth a lot, is it? Much higher rates can be obtained in the market, can't they?"

"Ah dearie, you don't understand the economics of it, markets may move down as well as up, this guarantee is a valuable fall-back."[14]

14. He turned out to be right: in the mid-90s market rates fell below guaranteed annuity rates when one insurer - *Equitable Life* - tried to deny its guaranty but the Law Lords held that it should honour its promise (July 2000).

Chapter Eleven

Mount clenched her fist dismissively, but Fingers seemed happy at this and even happier when his salesman added:

"And with BIG's expert management of investments, under Mr Lightman's inspirational leadership, of course, these policies should easily out-perform any occupational scheme."

The Mount pounced: "That can hardly be true after deduction of BIG's charges, can it?"

"Long-term, long-term!"

"And it is definitely untrue without the employer's contributions, isn't it?"

No reply.

She moved on: "Would you not agree that the principles of good selling practice adopted by the insurance industry generally, particularly following the Financial Services Act 1986, require warnings to be given to prospective policyholders of any adverse consequences?"

"That's a laugh! Warn the punters off! Not bloody likely in my experience - could seriously damage commission-income, couldn't it? Be reasonable!" Mr Hart appeared outraged. So did his Mr Lightman, although seemingly for different reasons since he intervened to suggest a settlement.

"We're a bit stuck here, Mr Parker," said Fingers in a concerned voice. "Revenue rules simply don't permit repayment of pensions money to members of schemes before their actual retirement, so I'm afraid we can't make a payment to you in any event. The money could in theory be transferred back to your firm's scheme but in practice that's not possible because of the unreasonable terms being imposed - you wanted to escape but it might be thought that that you're not wanted back! However, a practicable solution has just occurred to me: BIG could guarantee that at your retirement age - 65 isn't it? - the benefits under your personal pension will not be less than if you'd stayed in the occupational scheme. If they are, then we'll make up the difference. What do you say to that?"

Mrs Parker whined: "We wants some money now."

Her husband, however, asked Ollie what he thought and the Ombudsman opined gravely:

"In all the circumstances, Mr Lightman has in my judgment made a very reasonable suggestion. The guarantee must be put in writing, of course, and my office will able to tell you whether the terms appear satisfactory. So my considered advice is that you should accept the offer."

Eventually hands were shaken all round and Micky Hart even slapped a back or two - Fingers eyed a backside or two, but seemed intimidated by Mount's forbidding presence. The Parkers departed, still in their mackintoshes and appearing a little puzzled at the absence of money as well as of rain. Fingers and Hart left together but, Charlotte thought, rather at arm's length from each other. Ollie had declined persistent invitations to sup with the salesman. Another complaint had bitten the dust - settled by conciliation, both sides more or less satisfied.

Once the parties had safely left, Mount confronted the Ombudsman. "Why'd you let Fingers settle? We

Chapter Eleven

had that salesman on toast!" she demanded, standing above him.

Replied Ollie, sagely as well as bravely, it seemed to Charlotte:

"I had come to the conclusion that it was not a case of misselling but of missbuying. Not down to BIG, despite the deplorable Mr Hart. Punter Parker - sounds like a red Indian - really had only himself to blame, and Mrs P will be doing the blaming right now, I'll bet! He's lucky to get anything and actually Fingers' guarantee is pretty generous - although he wouldn't want me to say that, insurance companies are not supposed to be charitable institutions, and anyway he only made the offer for fear of worse after his salesman's performance."

Merciless Mount muttered: "You let him off the hook - I'd've screwed it right up his arse-hole."

Charlotte, affecting shock, sympathised. Maddie mimed the screwing, whilst chanting:

"Punter Parker picked a pack of pickled pricks!"

Not much later they all left to debrief at Stefano's. Ollie opened in epigrammatic mode:

"Occupational pensions are only as good as your employer, personal pensions as your insurer - the devil and the deep blue sea, which to choose? Conventional wisdom says pick the occupational but insurers do tend to have reliably deeper pockets than employers, well-lined at the punter's expense, so less likely to go bust - or pinch the funds!"

"I attempted to read Mr Parker's personal pension policy before the hearing," Charlotte said, "but hardly understood a word. It would've been no use asking me if it was better or worse than his firm's scheme. Haven't BIG heard of plain English?"

Mount loomed over her: "BIG's just the same as the rest of the long-term insurers - they don't want competition on the terms on offer, only between adverts. You've seen the posters, a beautifully sad black-clad widow caringly cared for as against a caricature of a pretty girl cleverly called Prudence, never mind Snow White. If punters could actually understand investment-linked policies, they might be able to choose the best buy for themselves, instead they either go for an advert or go to commission-hungry advisers."

"Didn't you tell me," Chip chipped in, "that these policies were deliberately obscure so as to hide the insurance companies' charges?"

"That too," said Mount. "But some of it doesn't seem obscure - there have been industry seminars on the skilled use of euphemisms and constructive semantics. My favourite is the one telling punters in plain English that 100% of their premiums will be invested, part of it in so-called 'capital units' - they never tumble that, under the small print, these pay the company's charges!"

Although listening Charlotte had been watching Ollie. He was talking to the waitress who had taken their orders. She had not seen her before: middle-aged rather than mini-skirted, her demeanour had remained severe and she had shouted at the barman. As Charlotte watched, however, the waitress smiled at Ollie.

"Ah ha, he wins again!" Maddie had also been

Chapter Eleven

watching, and added by way of explanation: "the Prof treats it as a challenge to chat-up every single waitress - or waiter come to that - until he gets them to smile, some are harder than others, but he rarely fails. Still don't know how he does it. Have you heard his chat-up lines? Prehistoric!"

Charlotte thought she knew: the medium not the message - Ollie always appeared to like the people he was talking to, especially women whom he obviously preferred, interested in their capabilities and concerns, sufficient small-talk, nevertheless listening and questioning instead of telling, but his secret lay in his smile - winsome! She knew what he would say: 'winsome, lose some', yet for her all of these characteristics of his were proving, if not actually irresistible, so far virtually unresisted. Or was he just profiting from her domestic situation, catching her bouncing on the rebound?

Chapter Twelve

Black And Blue Wednesday

Charlotte arrived early on Wednesday the fourth of April carrying a big brief-case concealing, she hoped, her over-night necessities and a change of suit.

Maddie was not deceived: "Working late eh, Lottie? Last night or this night? Home or away? Should only drop the 'C' not the 'Char' from your name!"

Oh very subtle, thought Charlotte, wondering how long it had taken her to think that one up - it was not her usual style of jolly insult. But in the circumstances better ignored, she decided.

"Maddie dearest, could I beg a favour?" Charlotte's answer to the questions was indirect but unambiguous. "I may be staying in town to-night with a friend Simon mightn't approve of, so I've told him you'll be putting me up - cover for me please? I'd always do the same for you if I could - if you ever need your back protecting, that is."

"Ah ha ha! Is this a professorial friend perchance?" crowed Maddie, evidently not spotting some too-subtle retaliation. "No, don't tell me, none of my business - of course, I'll cover for you, never fear, enjoy, enjoy!"

"I knew I could rely on your discretion," Charlotte simpered sweetly.

"Hey! Did I say that?" Maddie queried even more theatrically, "But it's true, I do respect confidences -

Chapter Twelve

never repeat them: tell one person at a time and then only once!"

Charlotte recognised a joke usually told of Oxford dons.

"By the way, drop the 'C' came from Marian," Maddie added.

At this point Ollie entered, seeking coffee and stifling any rude responses from Charlotte.

"Ready for the fray, Lot?" said he, clothed-all in green-oh - the corduroy three-piece suit was having an outing.

"Down at the Russell before 11.00 for more coffee with the little and bad."

"Then what?" she asked.

"We wait to be called - 'call the Ombudsman and his accomplice to answer whatever charges against them happen to take anyone's fancy'," he replied, histrionically. "Won't last long, we'll be expelled by lunch-time - not to feed with them, thank God, but to 'feed-back' - with her and the devilish duo, rather than Cocksie and the nobodies, thank God again!"

He departed carrying coffee in a mug bearing the familiar legend: 'AN OLD LAWYER NEVER DIES - HE JUST LOSES HIS APPEAL'.

"Why on earth the corduroy?" wondered Charlotte aloud.

"That's his country bumpkin get-up," burbled Maddie. "Always wears it for Council, helps his mad Professor act."

What act? Charlotte asked herself.

Ten-thirty on the dot, Marian 'Clerk to Council' put

his leer through the door.

"Ready to answer your summons Ms Angus?" said he, twitching his moustache officiously. "I'll show you the way."

"You go on," said she. "I'll follow with the Prof."

"Sure he won't lead you astray?" he sniggered departing importantly.

"Self-satisfying sod," muttered Maddie and started to sing the Robin Wood song.

Charlotte went to find Ollie. Surprised to see Mrs Arden at reception, telephone to hand, she asked:

"Where's Sarah?"

"Carrying Mr Wood's surplus papers down to Council," was the reply. "Needs all available assistance on Meeting days it seems - not used to doing anything for himself, I suppose."

Charlotte thought she caught a whiff of unanticipated asperity.

Ten-forty on the next dot, Ollie left the building with Charlotte in his slip-stream. Neither carried any papers.

"Be unprepared is my motto," he had said, untruthfully she knew, having experience of him doing his homework and saying pompously, as *Rommel* did, that time spent in reconnaissance is never wasted.

"Better to make it up than look it up. Don't want Council members poking their snotty noses into case files, not their bloody business. Bad enough that they have the temerity to criticise our decisions given the depths of their ignorance and prejudice."

"So what part do we play to-day?" she had asked.

Chapter Twelve

"Sycophantic respecters of their extraordinary wisdom and expertise, undertaking to take appropriate account of every whimsical word falling simultaneously from the tops of their heads and the backs of their necks. Takes great patience and tolerance."

Not practising but letting-off pre-emptive steam, she had thought.

"But got to be suffered, if I want reappointment, that is - first two years up soon and the BIG boys will definitely try to get rid of me, so the rest must be kept flattered, at least for the time being."

They had hurried off along Southampton Row.

Ten-fifty on the penultimate dot, Ollie and Charlotte, both breathless, reached the Russell, an impressively plush establishment which had somehow survived attempts to convert it into a modern, characterless hotel of the convenience chain variety. In an elegantly and comfortably furnished ante-room, coffee and biscuits were being consumed noisily by Council members preparatory to the Meeting as if thirst and starvation threatened during it. Charlotte saw Arms and Fingers haranguing, and being harangued, by persons as yet unknown to her: two medium-sized middle-aged men in matching brown suits and a smaller woman of 'late youth' clad in a bright blue trouser suit with such wide shoulder pads that she looked like a tethered kite. Arms and Fingers each greeted Ollie's arrival with rather wolfish smiles, Charlotte thought, whilst the others ignored him and examined her.

However Lady Cocks welcomed them, hand-bag in one hand, chocolate biscuit in the other:

"Here you are, Oliver, at last, and Ms Angus dear, as you want to be called, I hear. Don't hold with gels using maiden names after marriage myself. We must talk about it later, see what should be done. You might think better of it then. Now I need to speak to the Ombudsman before the Meeting."

"Yes Chairman," smiled that short-term sycophant. "How can I assist?"

"It's not a matter of assistance, Oliver," said his Chairman sternly. "I thought it right to notify you in advance of an item of 'any other business' that Robert Walker has requested. It has been decided, after proper discussion with me of course, that the office should move to Winchester."

No longer breathless but for once speechless, eventually Ollie gasped:

"What on earth for?"

He was shaken Charlotte saw.

"Primarily we had in mind enhancing the lifestyles of our staff, including yourself naturally, as well as your successor. Much nicer place to live and work rather than travelling every day into Central London, nearer the BIG head-office in Bournemouth too. An incidental advantage, as you will appreciate, will be escaping from the exorbitant rentals being exacted for City offices. With a rent review imminent, commercial sense demands that less expensive premises be sought, with room for expansion, somewhere such as Winchester. No doubt everyone will be delighted to learn of this beneficial development. But we can't talk about it now, it's time for the Meeting!"

Chapter Twelve

So, on the appointed dot, Lady Cocks called out with penetration and authority:

"Shall we move in and begin, it is eleven o'clock!"

Handbag held in her right-hand, as if a symbol of office, she moved ahead. As the Council Members removed themselves in response like masticating sheep into their Private Meeting and/or Dining Room, where Marian awaited. Sarah at his side, Ollie did not look delighted.

"Very clever," he sighed, sinking into a sofa, "Bob's been nobbled. Marginalise the office. Make me commute out of London or else resign. The girls won't travel to Winchester and nor, I suppose, will you."

Charlotte shook her head miserably.

"Whose idea would it be?" she asked, sitting beside him.

"Fingers probably, backed by Arms. Failing to get Bob to abandon the scheme because of the loss of face factor, he's come up with some brilliant lateral thinking. Well it'll probably be the end of the Insurance Ombudsman experiment as we know and love it," said Ollie sadly. "We'd better start looking for alternative employment."

"Will the rest of Council agree to the move," asked Charlotte.

"Bound to, they've never yet stood up to Cocksey bearing BIG's Bob's bountiful commands. The only consolation is that I'll no longer need to be patient and tolerant with that bunch of self-important idiots!"

Suffering fools is something he'll gladly see happening, instead of do himself, she thought.

"Will you go back home to your wife and your university?" Charlotte asked.

"Can't quite do that," Ollie replied. "Took early retirement on generous terms, government funded, sort of voluntary redundancy, culling the older experienced dons and freezing new appointments - they're all the same age now, growing old together. And I've got used to living down here away from trouble and strife."

"So what will you do?" she persisted, thinking more about what she would do - back to litigation practice beckoned, a proper job, but she wondered where.

"Well I could go to a privately funded university, like the one at Buckingham, and still keep my enhanced early pension. Funnily enough, approaches have already been made. And I have 'the book'!"

"A novel?" she exclaimed, "Bet it's a bodice-ripper!"

"No no," said he. "A practitioner's textbook - I edit *Ant on Abstracts*, have done for years, loose-leaf, three fat volumes, a profitable treadmill, keeps me in the style to which I've become accustomed!"

"But who or what is Ant?"

"He was a Yorkshire solicitor whose office notes on perusing abstracts of title and conveyancing practice were first published just over a century ago. He's long since dead, but his book lives on, though I doubt if he'd recognise it now - only one slim volume in 1888."

"And it still sells?" Charlotte asked.

"I'll say," replied Ollie. "Very popular with practitioners - and with the publisher, nice big earner. They held a party last year to celebrate the 100th anniversary of its first publication. Got the venerable

Chapter Twelve

Ned Oldhorse QC along - nick-named 'new gee-gee' at prep school, still known to contemporaries as 'the great newgee' - leading dinosaur of the Chancery Bar. The plan was he'd say a few valedictory words while a cake, made in the shape of an 'A' and iced in the emetic, greeny-blue colours of the book, was wheeled in ablaze with 100 just-lit candles. The moment was memorable! The heat from the candles set off the fire alarms - sirens and sprinklers almost literally drowned every word!"

Then another memorable moment occurred. The Dining and/or Meeting Room door flew open and Lady Cocks erupted, brandishing her handbag and slammed the door behind her. Red-faced with fury, chins trembling, she glared with overt hostility at Ollie and Charlotte:

"How dare they?" she bellowed.

No answer seemed safe and, after a long minute, she turned towards her hat and coat, hung with others, which she scattered, on an elaborate stand by the entrance to the ante-room.

"Despicable disloyalty!" she added, pinning her hat dangerously into her purple wig. The colour clash with her current complexion struck Charlotte as alarming.

"After all I've done for everyone!"

She flung on her coat whilst regarding the offending Ollie and his moll accusingly. They shrank a little into their ornate sofa. Her ladyship departed with dramatic suddenness, crying out, somewhat pathetically Charlotte thought:

"Wait 'till I tell Bob!"

They were still looking at each other in stunned

silence when the door opened again and Sarah emerged rather cautiously. Seeing no sign of Lady Cocks, she closed the door carefully behind her.

"What the Hell has happened?" asked Ollie.

Sarah came and sat by them.

"Ooh, it's ever so exciting! On the agenda, after last minutes and matters arising, Robbie'd had me type 'Election of Chairman' - Cocksey's two years were up, see. 'Well', she says, with her 'ha ha'," - Sarah began to reveal a talent for mimicry - "'This comprehends re-election, of course, and as there are no nominations. . .' Then that Mr Laddie says 'Chairman, I'd like to nominate Mrs Freeman to succeed you' and Mr Blackburne says 'seconded'."

"Ah ha, an ambush!" Ollie said nodding. "What next?"

"Cocksey says: 'What, what? But she's not been nominated in writing, two weeks notice, that's right Clerk, isn't it?' 'No-one has been nominated' says Robbie, 'Not even you, Chairman'. 'Well, Frankie doesn't want to stand, do you?' says Cocksey. However that one says, all prissy faced: 'So sorry, Chairman, but if my Council colleagues consider it appropriate I must respect their wishes'. Then she goes and nominates Mr Blackburne. Mr Laddie says 'seconded'. Then Mr Blackburne nominates Mr Laddie and Mrs Freeman says 'seconded'!"

"So they're all candidates, obviously a conspiracy," observed Ollie. "What about BIG's boys, though, surely they said something?"

"Oh yes," Sarah carries on. "Mr Lightman says 'Let's be sensible' and nominates Cocksey. Mr Scott says

Chapter Twelve

'seconded' and asks 'Will you three withdraw now?' They all shake their heads and Robbie says: 'There'll have to be an election, I'd better check the rules.' Then Cocksey stands up, says 'It would be utterly demeaning, I've never been so insulted,' grabs her handbag and slams out of the door. Mr Lightman says: 'The MD won't like this' and proposes Council adjourns. Mr Scott seconds that but the other three all say 'no', and Mr Laddie says he's vice-chairman and he'll run the election. Then Mr Lightman looks at me and says to Robbie I shouldn't be there, so I had to leave. Shame really, wonder what's going on now."

"Presumably they're choosing a new Chairman," said Ollie. "And we'll find out who fairly soon - we should run a book!"

Turning to Charlotte he added: "Doubt if they'll get to any other business."

"You mean the move to Winchester will be off?" she replied, brightening.

"Probably only postponed, what do you think Sarah?"

"Winchester? Do me a favour! I'm going to use that 'phone, got to talk to my friend about to-night," was the response.

She has a short excitement-span, thought Charlotte, at least so far as Council is concerned.

At this point the Meeting/Dining Room door opened and Marian the Clerk and Manager emerged.

"Professor Goodman, Ms Angus," said he with no vestige of a leer. "Council will see you both now."

Ollie stood up: "The suspensefulness is terrific! Come on Lot, let's face the music and dance!"

"Last tango in Holborn?" she enquired.

As they entered, Charlotte behind Ollie saw a flash of blue at the end of a dining-table.

"So you won, Frankie, you're our new Chairman!" cried Ollie, "Ha ha! Congratulations!"

"Thank you Oliver," said she, looking Charlotte thought like the mouse that got the cheese. "But it's Frances if you please and I shall be correctly called 'Chair', Hugh becomes 'Vice-Chair', and similarly you will be referred to as 'Ombud'."

All Ollie managed was: "So you'll become Free, not Freeman, will you, Frances? Can I be your Ombuddy?"

"Such facetiousness is unacceptable," he was told sharply. "This Meeting is about to adjourn for lunch. I have proposed that it be reconvened as soon as possible over a weekend at a residential centre away from central London. That will afford a badly-needed opportunity for us to re-examine the fundamentals of the scheme, to re-consider management controls, to establish principles for casework guidance - by Council for the instruction of Assistants - and to achieve team-bonding for ourselves in a less-pressurised atmosphere."

She looked up from her notes and smiled at Ollie, without ulterior intent Charlotte thought, and continued:

"Your presence will be expected throughout, as will that of Robin, but Ms Angus's attendance will not be required, nor will that of your assistant, Sarah is it Robin?"

Marian the Manager nodded, gritted teeth beneath a near-leer. Charlotte looked at the expressions around

Chapter Twelve

the table - had they all been listening truly appalled?

The door was knocked and opened simultaneously. BIG's unmistakable Bob loomed in, not even pretending to offer humble apologies:

"Hope I'm not interrupting."

He scrutinised the scenario:

"Or am I late for lunch? Hello everyone - but where's our Jenny?"

Fingers hardly hesitated: "She's gone, MD, no longer Chairman - they've elected Mrs Freeman instead."

Bob took this in bleakly for a while. Then smiled without humour at Frances the Chair, who flared her nostrils and flexed her shoulder-pads back at him.

"So you're now well on the way to achieving your ambitions, young Frankie," he observed.

She responded, fiercely furious: "I simply have aspirations for the value-effective operation in future of the Ombud scheme, something we surely all share."

"We'll have to see, won't we?" Bob replied with, Charlotte thought, ambivalent menace.

Ollie and Charlotte, never invited to sit, gladly left them to their lunch. Marian and Sarah joined them on the walk back to the office - could she have spotted them surreptitiously holding hands, wondered Charlotte. Ollie asked about the election. Breaching confidentiality without further encouragement or any sign of restraint, Marian the Council Clerk outlined events:

"They decided against a show of hands, so I prepared voting papers for a secret ballot - Fingers and Arms, being from BIG, were not eligible and they abstained from everything, so it was a three-horse race. First ballot they tied for first place - one vote each, their own I supposed. Second ballot two for Frankie wankie, one for Laddie waddie - Blackers must have put his cross in the wrong box, stupid sod!"

"So Bob's not your uncle and Madame wins a huge vote of confidence," concluded Ollie, "We've gone from headmistress to milk-monitor."

"Yeah," sighed Marian, his patroness's displacement had wiped the leer from his face. "I just can't stand that suit - arrogant in style, colour and content!"

Power-dressing - reserved for men, thought Charlotte somewhat sourly, but asked:

"If she doesn't like Free, why doesn't she use her maiden name like me?"

Both Ollie and Marian laughed and the former explained:

"She can't at this stage of her ambitions - it's the same as BIG Bob's, Walker, - it might be thought she'd been a beneficiary of nepotism and that wouldn't be politically correct!"

Chapter Thirteen

Wednesday Aftermath

Reaching the office Ollie gathered his girls and ushered them off to Stefano's for 'feed-back, feed-up and drink-down', as he put it. His account of Council's revolting meeting would not prove conducive to productivity. Ollie gave good feed-back - blood on the carpet featured frequently - but the news for the scheme seemed to all to be terminal: sooner rather than later Frankie Free's blatant ambition, together with Arms' and Fingers' persistent hostility, must persuade BIG's Bob to end the experiment. So jaw jaw, not work work, was always likely to be the order of the afternoon.

Returning to the office, sensibly sober since Ollie and Charlotte had prudently practised moderation prior to the evening's wine-tasting, they found Frances the Chair awaiting with a frozen face.

"At last," she said. "Oliver kindly call all the staff together in the Council Chamber, secretarial as well as Assistants. I shall address them."

So soon Chip and Mount, Maddie and Charlotte, Marian and Sarah, Mrs Arden and Ollie, the complete crew, stood around the table at which sat a blue suit with wide shoulders. She flared her nostrils and began reading a prepared text:

"Now that I'm in charge of running the scheme" - Ollie and Marian glanced at each other, exchanging extreme sympathy - "changes will be made. The structure, staffing and working methods employed by the office must all be reviewed by management consultants. Their report will form the basis for a business plan to be implemented during the coming year. Computer facilities will be installed on expert advice. Productivity targets will be agreed. Service standards will be set and publicised as a bench-mark for handling complaints against the scheme, all of which will be referred to me for investigation. You must all buy in to a mission statement and agree the values to be applied in the office's dealings with insurers and customers. These shall include -

independence through the exercise of impartiality

efficiency stemming from professionalism and expertise

accessibility based upon the use of plain language, helpfulness and timely responses to requests.

I trust I make myself clear. Any questions?"

Charlotte wondered who would dare as a stunned silence settled on the staff. However, she had reckoned without Mrs Arden:

"Yes I have a question - who on Earth are you?"

This seemed to nonplus the wee Free, at least she offered no immediate answer. Ollie leapt to the rescue:

"Meet the new Chair of Council, Mrs Arden, successor to Lady Cocks by virtue of an election at which, I understand, she won 100% more votes than the runner-up. Her name is Mrs Freeman."

He turned to her: "Now Chair, if you've finished

the manifesto, perhaps you'd permit the Ombud and his Assists to get on with their casework. As you know we do this independently of Council. Let me show you off the premises."

Immensely to Charlotte's surprise, the new Chair allowed herself to be gestured out without another word. As with most of his waving-down at the oral hearing, Ollie gave good gesture and his waving-out worked. Since she said nothing, the Chair seemed to have shot her bolt for the time-being, or she may have run out of prepared text.

The rest of the staff also sidled out in silence. Maddie looked at Charlotte: "Bloody Hell!"

Chapter Fourteen

Winning Wednesday

After a few desultory attempts to concentrate on her cases, Charlotte was relieved as well as a little excited when Ollie eventually collected her.

"Time to go, Lot," said he.

Maddie had already left. It was nearly six o'clock.

"We've comfortable time to walk round to Chancery Lane."

She picked up her big bag, filled with overnight things.

"What about this?" she asked, feeling prematurely committed and maturely compromised.

"Ah ha, leave that here for the time being - I have a cunning plan!"

And I know the bottom line, she thought, not very perceptively but actually quite presciently.

"Not what you're thinking," he added. "It's to do with misleading that private eye you told me about, assuming he's still on the job."

"No other plans?" she asked, affecting innocence.

"Well maybe one or two," said he, trying to put thoughts of her bottom out of his mind.

They arrived at The Law Society's Hall, via Lincoln's Inn's Fields, talking a bit not touching at all, comfortably before half-past.

"Best be in good time, get good places," Ollie observed seriously.

Chapter Fourteen

Hanging their coats in the unattended ground-floor cloakroom -

"It's alright, said Ollie obscurely. "Only estate agents' furs get pinched from here."

- they hurriedly ascended impressive stairs to the first-floor hall where the wine was to be tasted. She had been there before; its day-job was dining-room and its decor splendidly vulgar - *nouveaux riches* as against the ancien regime of the Inns of Court, preserved for barristers and judges, gentlemen not tradesmen, however prosperous.

They were not the first. Ollie hastened to take two chairs in the middle of a side table facing towards the top table. She saw there were some fifteen places, pieces of paper and two glasses at each, six uncorked bottles at either end of the table with two empty jugs, two plates of biscuits and two plates of tiny cheese cubes down the middle.

"Here we can see, hear and, more important, almost always get a fair share."

He explained that the bottles to be tasted would start at one end, and had to be shared amongst fifteen so that, if the first people helped themselves to too much, the other end lost out. Then they would make up for it when the next bottle started at their end. Nasty scenes, near fisticuffs, certainly biscuit throwing, had been known to break out - difficult initially for solicitors unaccustomed to overt acts of hostility and ostensibly anxious not to distract the speakers, but the greater their consumption the less their inhibitions. The Chairman had even felt called upon to thump the table and shout for order as near-end and far-end relations threatened to conduct themselves unbecomingly.

"However," said Ollie, "those in the middle should intercept a decent sample safely so long as they keep their heads down and out of any battle between the ends."

"Professor Goodman, you probably won't remember me, but I was one of your students more years ago than I care to mention," a stylishly-dressed business-woman, bottle-blond hair, wearing winged glasses and extravagant earrings, greeted Ollie.

"Of course I remember you," Ollie leapt to his feet, "Janet Smith, as ever was, goodish degree in '71, I think it was, despite being President of the Law Students' Association, started an undergraduate magazine carrying subversive caricatures of the staff. You've hardly changed at all - what are you doing now?"

"Company lawyer, specialising in pension schemes," she replied.

"Is that ah interesting?" he asked.

"Not really, lots of detailed documentation and complicated tax rules, but it's profitable - I'm an equity partner at Oppenheimers in the City."

"Oh dear! I'm always meeting former students who've made their fortune despite my teaching!"

"Or because of it - I learnt pragmatism from your tutorials," she said, and Charlotte wondered whether she intended a compliment.

"You're still at the University, then?" Janet continued.

"Left two years ago, desperately needed a change from academic life, if one can call it that, became the

CHAPTER FOURTEEN

BIG Insurance Ombudsman - let me introduce my one and only legal expert, Charlotte Angus - also a solicitor - Janet Smith, an old student of mine."

She won't like the 'old', thought Charlotte, saying: "People call me Lottie, was he always so tactful?"

"Usually just rude - or forthright - about everything and everyone. The students loved it!"

And some of them loved him, Charlotte speculated.

"Anyway, I'm Janet Sloss these days and I'd better go back to my ever-loving husband before he suspects something. Look, let's be in touch, have a meal or something."

She left leaving Ollie with a business card and Charlotte with a brief nod.

"Lottie, it is, isn't it? What are you doing here?" came a voice from the past.

"Graham!" she said, pleased, "I'm with him - my new boss, Professor Oliver Goodman, BIG's insurance ombudsman - Ollie meet Graham Lawrence, my old boss, the litigation partner in charge of personal injuries cases."

"Nominally, nominally," said Graham, shaking hands with Ollie. "Lottie was always in charge of everything herself, I just agreed with whatever she suggested."

"I'm already familiar with the role," replied Ollie.

"But when did you go back to work? Are you full-time? Why didn't you let us know?" Graham questioned Charlotte rather peremptorily before remembering where they were and enquiring with concern:

"And how are the twins coming along? They must be three now - Bill and Ben, flower-pot men, eh?"

"Dan and Benjy," she corrected his customary jocular mistake, laughing as if she had not heard it before.

"And what about you, Lottie? You look well!"

At that point, fortunately she thought, proceedings showed signs of commencing so Graham abandoned cross-examination, saying:

"Must go back to my guest, nice to meet you, Professor er Goldstein, let's be in touch Lottie. Bye!"

He scuttled off, nearly middle-aged, long-nosed, black-haired but balding and quivering with nervous energy.

"Not a Lot to him?" Ollie asked.

"Never," she said, affecting a shudder.

"And Janet - old flame?"

"Not mine," said he, somewhat hastily, "She was the Faculty Flame!"

The top table had become occupied by three disparate individuals. One of them, an untidy genial bear of a man, evidently the Society's Chairman, was attempting amiably to make himself heard. Eventually the noise from the tables subsided sufficiently. He was heard to welcome everyone, "especially our visitors from one of Her Majesty's far-flung colonies." Apparently the American Title Insurance Lawyers' Association was holding its annual conference in London and had invited The Law Society's conveyancing sub-committee, including the Chairman, to participate in a session on profitable practices. A reciprocal invitation to the tasting had been extended to any wine enthusiasts, a couple of dozen accepting. Looking around their table, Charlotte realised that they were not, contrary to Ollie's

CHAPTER FOURTEEN

explanatory predictions, entirely surrounded by soberly-attired solicitors with suburban spouses: many of their drinking companions were only too obviously on a jolly holiday from the US of A. She hoped they sampled by the rules - Ollie would be angry if he failed to taste at least enough of the wine.

To mark the visit of "our erstwhile transatlantic allies", the Chairman continued, the Committee had decided to use some of the Society's surplus funds to subsidise an unique vertical tasting of the exceptional premier-cru claret, *Chateau Figeac*. It was unique particularly because the Chateau's proprietors, Monsieur et Madame Desbordes had graciously agreed to be present and talk us through the vintages. He nodded towards the elderly couple seated beside him and led a round of applause.

The elderly couple looked puzzled and remained seated. The Chairman nodded at them pointedly and clapped again, this time alone. The elderly couple looked at each other and remained seated. The Chairman smiled genially at the audience then bent and whispered for a while into the elderly gentleman's ear. Monsieur Desbordes then turned to Madame Desbordes and whispered into her painted mask of a face for a while with agitated hand and eyebrow language. Through her make-up, she appeared to give better than she got. At last, with unconcealed relief the Chairman could sit because one of the proprietors stood. Erect, tall, thin and white-haired, his small nose, ruddy face and spectacles instead of moustache precluded comparisons with General de Gaule. But his speaking style did not. He declaimed, with pride and pomposity, at length and in French.

As loath to offend a distinguished guest as to confess incomprehension, the assembled tasters, legally eager and notionally expert, took quite a few minutes to become obviously and audibly restless. They started by eating the cheese and biscuits. Then they began talking in low voices amongst themselves. Charlotte, daring to display ignorance, asked Ollie what was meant by a tasting being 'vertical'.

"Same chateau, different years," said he, a little too cryptically, she thought. "Horizontal involves comparing wines of the same year from different chateaux. We're going to taste the '87 *Figeac* first then the '85 and work back, according to the tasting list, to the '59, missing out a few inferior years. The younger vintages will hardly be drinkable, the tannin you know, and the oldest could be over the top, though with this Chateau I doubt it. Anyway, allowing for age, the comparisons should be instructive."

As to what, she wondered.

Monsieur Desbordes was still talking to himself without, so far as could be told, instructing those still listening to pour the first two bottles. He seemed to be dwelling on the temperature at which the grapes were picked, if Charlotte's A-level French could be believed, instead of starting the race. However the Americans must have had a thirsty day or another engagement - or both - for they cracked and anticipated the instruction. Pouring themselves generous measures, they passed the first two bottles, the '87 and the '85,

CHAPTER FOURTEEN

round the table. They swirled and sniffed before sipping. Then spat and tipped the rest into the jugs, declaring their strong preference for Californian Masson.

The Chairman rapped the table and displayed disappointed disapproval. His disappointment increased when one of the Americans, self-appointed or not a leader, announced their immediate departure - a theatre experience was next on their tight schedule, *The Mousetrap* that most intellectual of shows. They were excused and Charlotte observed that Ollie and one or two others did not share the Chairman's disappointment:

"Good riddance, now there'll be more than enough for us," he whispered penetratingly.

When the Americans had made good their scheduled retreat, the painted bird-like Madame Desbordes spoke fiercely to her spouse who sat down instantly. She then led the remaining solicitors through the rest of the comparative tasting not only briskly but in fluent English. It went extremely well, not least on account of the unusually ample samples consumed on all but the top-table of a dozen bottles of, as Ollie pontificated, "a stylish, rich yet elegant wine." Audience bonhomie abounded. Solicitors spoke to non-clients, wittily and without introductions. A few clever, clever questioners were politely deflated. The Chairman benevolently reminisced a bit about the St Emilion hospitality that, once upon a time, he personally had been privileged to enjoy before calling for appreciation to be expressed in the usual way. That meant clapping - ordinarily sedate, Ollie explained, but on this excessively liquid occasion a standing ovation occurred spontaneously, from all those still able to stand. Monsieur et Madame Desbordes appeared extraordinarily surprised and slightly gratified.

Chapter fifteen

Wednes-Night

No wine left, nor any for sale, Ollie and Charlotte departed without delay. Collecting their coats from the cloakroom, Charlotte was sure she had spotted Timmy Lloyd amongst the solicitors and their spouses in the lobby. But he was nowhere to be seen as they went out into Chancery Lane.

"We must pick up your bag," said Ollie.

Rather unsteadily, they retraced their route from the office back around Lincoln's Inn's Fields. She told Ollie about spotting Timmy. Somewhat irresponsibly, he put his arm round her and said:

"Remember I have a cunning plan!"

She giggled and put her arm round him.

Untangling as they reached Kingsway, they carefully crossed the various trafficky roads between them and the office entrance. Charlotte looked round quickly. She nearly fell over and saw no sign of Timmy. Another look - did someone dodge out of sight into the shoe shop doorway? Ollie let them in and re-locked the street door behind them.

"He'll be watching for us to come out," she observed.

"Let him."

They climbed the stairs to the scheme's offices - apart from the narrow stairwell all was dark as well as silent and empty. Ollie thumbed in the combination, 0pened the door and entered noisily. He then switched on several lights - corridor, his room and Mrs Arden's as well as the Council Chamber.

"Fetch your bag and follow me," he whispered conspiratorially and apparently soberly.

Leaving all the lights on, Ollie opened an obscure door at the end of a short passage off from reception and used to store broken chairs. Charlotte saw that the door was marked 'Fire Escape'. Shutting the door behind them, he shone a torch and she found they were descending a grandiose curved stairway towards wide swing doors round the edge of which came light and the smell of Italian cooking. They pushed cautiously into and less cautiously through the Spaghetti House's kitchen. Ollie waved a greeting to the chefs, called out:

"Ciao Mario," to the head waiter, adding: "Back soon - not a word to anyone!"

Then he led her hastily out of the staff exit and dangerously round the taxis and across Vernon Place into Bloomsbury Square.

"Your private eye is in for a long wait!" he announced triumphantly, putting both his arms round her - the Square was not well lit. She laughed as she thought: silly, clever person. Seduced away from sense by the circumstances, they kissed at last, instinctively and closely, careless of watchers, she still clutching her bag.

He's kissed before, occurred to her, he knows what to do with his tongue.

Untangling again, they crossed Southampton Row and went down a passage to reach Great Ormond Street Hospital.

CHAPTER FIFTEEN

"This is my normal route home to the flat," said Ollie.

"What! Including the Bloomsbury Square diversion?" exclaimed Charlotte, vaguely wondering about the 'normal'.

He only smiled.

"Ten minute walk from the office. Trinity Court in Gray's Inn Road - do you know it?"

She shook her head happily, despite knowing another little lecture was about to be delivered, the sedative effect of the wine, no doubt.

"The block featured in that notorious 1985 film *Mona Lisa* starring Michael Caine and Bob Hoskins - they were seen drinking in the corner pub. The call-girl, beautifully played by Cathy Tyson, was supposed to live there."

Ollie paused apparently in recollection.

"We could watch the video sometime."

Not to-night, I'll bet, Charlotte giggled to herself.

"The real residents," he continued, "were warned about the filming: 'there will be human emotion in the lifts' - apparently there was tomato ketchup and screaming everywhere! The block was clearly identified in the film - not sure whether it put the flat's value up or down, but taxi drivers always know where Trinity Court is. And here we are."

They were outside a tattily decorated eight-storey purpose built block containing a hundred or so small flats, judging by the bell numbers on the entryphone.

"I'm sixth-floor back, quiet, sun in the morning, good view of the graveyard - it's built on the site of a church, devil-worship in the basement, I believe."

They entered an antique lift with old-fashioned metal concertina-grill doors at each side through which the occupants could see and be seen as they ascended or descended caged like trapped animals.

"These lifts - there's another at the back of the building - were the reason for the film's location here. There was a spectacular knife fight through the doors. I normally climb the stairs, for my health, but we've arrived safely."

Where's my health warning when I need it? thought Charlotte. Holding her arm he led her down a dark brown corridor to the back of the block, opened the front door of Flat No. 69 and said:

"Come in Lot."

My time's up, she told herself, still tingling with alcohol and excitement, but only saying:

"Is this where the call-boy lives?"

"Let me give you a guided tour," said Ollie, hanging their coats on pegs behind the door. "Thirty seconds at most. To your left, first the bathroom."

Tiny, no windows, lavatory and bath with electric shower, but usable by two, one at a time, thought Charlotte.

"Next door, the bedroom."

Slightly less tiny, wide window, floor-space virtually filled with a pine double bed, barely room for an upright chair, a small chest and a narrow wardrobe, but also usable, two at a time, she thought, leaving her overnight bag by the bed. There was also a convector heater which Ollie switched on, saying:

"Don't want us to catch cold."

Chapter Fifteen

"Ahead, the living-stroke-dining room with kitchen alcove," said Ollie the guide.

Not tiny at all, rectangular with a kitchenny-equipped bit at one end and a dining-table - already laid for two - in front of a matching wide window at the other end. Small convertible sofa, big easy chair, bookshelves, night-storage heaters, TV and video with half-a dozen pictures on the walls - all framed cartoons and caricatures. Colour scheme red or white throughout.

Comfortable accommodation, she thought, for one with a house elsewhere.

"And that's all, apart from the balcony," he indicated a door beside the window, "Not large but fine for a leisurely breakfast in the early morning sun - looks across the graveyard into the nurses' hostel, they wave at me!"

"Wave back, I expect you mean," she dared to say.

"Now, now, don't be cheeky, at the University I often had female students beating at my study door."

"Yes, yes, I know, but you never let them out!"

They laughed together at another familiarity.

There's nothing like an old joke, she thought, perhaps I'm the punchline.

"Well now, Lot," said Ollie. "What about a light snack to soak up the wine? I've got some smoked salmon and salad, with brown bread, also some rather more interesting cheese than The Law Society's cubed variety - it's always cooking cheddar!"

He went to the kitchen end, opened the fridge and brought back a bottle of champagne plus two champagne glasses.

"No more red just now - we can be washing the tasting away with this while I get the food out, should be alright, it's a '76 Moët. I've some specially selected Burgundy for later."

If we're still capable, thought Charlotte, but then wondered of what.

They drank, ate and talked for a while, like companionable colleagues, but looking more and more into each other's eyes and eventually holding hands. Then Ollie said:

"Lot, I think I've begun to love you a little too much."

"Me too," said Charlotte. "Oh you know what I mean."

He stood and kissed her. Soon she pushed him away and said:

"I must go to the bathroom."

"Me too," he said. "I mean, you first."

"Bathroom's vacant," she called, sneaking into the bedroom full of illicit expectations of an horizontal tasting. Her own little wittiscm had been appealing to her all evening.

When he followed her into the bedroom, her clothes were on the chair and she was under his duvet. She regarded him gravely:

"Don't think I get my kit off for anyone."

"I don't," he said, not smiling but undressing hurriedly.

What's behind the green cord? she sang to herself as his country suit hit the floor - she thought she knew: a rather rotund middle-aged man who wanted his wicked way with her. Perhaps more stocky than portly,

CHAPTER FIFTEEN

she saw, and quite a hairy chest. Also circumcised!

He placed his spectacles on the window-sill, skilfully dimmed the bed-side light and pushed in under the duvet, held her and kissed her again, and again. She kissed back, deeply, and held him, tightly.

Then she thought anxiously: Where's his erection?

Ollie lay on his side and turned her towards him. Still holding her, one hand stroked her back gently, feeling along her silky skin and delicate contours. The hand moved down to her bottom, felt her less delicate curves, stroking all the while, at first tenderly then more vigorously, around and between.

There's the erection, she suddenly realised.

"In vino very fat arse," Ollie murmured.

"Shut up and keep stroking," she ordered.

So he did, for quite a while.

Maybe this is the bottom line, she thought.

Then he suddenly turned her onto her back, knelt beside her and kissed her nipples, held her breasts and pinched her nipples and licked them energetically and bit them a bit. Through her surprise and pleasure Charlotte thought: that's two out of three erogenous zones. As if reacting to her thought, he smoothly moved head and hands down her body to do very much the same - kissing, holding, pinching and especially licking - right between her legs.

"Ooh! My God!" she cried, no longer thinking. "Fuck me!"

So he did but too soon. . .

'Bang, bang, bang!' Ombudsman *interruptus*.

"It's someone at the front door," said Ollie, irritatedly.

"Let them go away," said Charlotte, frustratedly.

They heard shouting: "Fire, fire - everybody out!"

"Oh sod it," muttered Ollie, leaping from the bed into the passage. "I can smell smoke."

Charlotte joined him wrapped in the duvet. The letter box opened:

"Emergency - vacate the building!" came a shout accompanied by more banging and some smoke.

Ollie grabbed his coat and opened the door. A bright flash greeted them - a photographer's flash. Blinded for an instant, they heard a voice say:

"Fank you kindly, Sir and Madame, an' wot abaht a smile this time?"

Another flash but they had shut their eyes and so could open them in time to see a tall figure with balaclavered features carrying a large camera turn to escape away down the stairs beside the lift.

There was no fire only a piece of burnt newspaper. Enquiring heads were poking angrily out of other doors.

Ollie called out cheerily: "Seems to have been a false alarm. Or a practical joke. Back to bed and off to sleep everyone!" He pushed Charlotte inside and closed the door.

She said. "That was Timmy. How did he get in?"

"Easy, I'm afraid - intruders are always getting in - they just ring entryphone bells until someone expecting a visitor opens the door."

"So much for your cunning plans."

"Well, one of them worked," said he.

"Very funny," she said. "What shall we do now?"

Chapter Fifteen

"Another bottle of bubbly, then back to bed," he suggested.

So that was what they did.

Chapter Sixteen

Morning After

Charlotte's satiated slumber, or maybe drunken stupor she thought, was disturbed by Ollie, this time seeking information:

"Tea, coffee, with or without, and/or grapefruit juice?"

"Tea, no milk, no sugar - juice and coffee later," she replied. "But what time is it?"

"Gone half-seven - I'll make tea then you can have an hour's doze while I use the bathroom."

"What on earth do you do for an hour?"

"Shave and shower, shave and shower I'm not a fast-mover in the morning at the best of times and this morning for reasons well known to you I feel distinctly sluggish," he explained, unconvincingly she thought.

"Forget tea and get back into bed immediately," she ordered. "I'll speed you up."

So he did and she did.

Breakfasting by the window, coffee with Cox's apples and a little truckle of Cheddar, both in dressing-gowns, Charlotte said slyly as well as shyly:

"I thought you might not like me."

"But you're really beautiful Lot," said Ollie enthusiastically, "Even sexier than I imagined."

"Oh you've been imagining sex have you, you dirty devil!"

Chapter Sixteen

"Of course," he said. "An Ombudsman's gotta do what an Ombudsman's gotta do! But it was me I was worried about, especially at first, but all's well that ends well."

"Was that the end then?" she asked.

"No, only the end of the beginning or the beginning of the end, whatever and whenever it may be," he responded, not seriously she hoped.

"Which brings us nicely to your private eye," he continued, seriously she feared.

"Not mine," she objected, "Timmy works for Arms."

"Be that as it may, the consequence is that we'll almost certainly be threatened with exposure. Will you mind?"

He paused: "The exposure, that is, not the threat."

"Not much, I think," she replied after thought, "But Ollie, it's you Arms is out to get. If you give in to him on one or two decisions, surely he'll keep quiet?"

"Can't do that, must have some self-respect. When the threat breaks, the Ollie won't fall!" he declaimed. "I'll just have to suffer the slings and arrows of outraged Beryl!"

"She'll hospitalise you," sighed Charlotte. "But I'll come and visit - we are in this together, aren't we?"

"I certainly hope so, silver lining if we emerge as a couple, though you must have developed an obsession with older men - you're not becoming a grey-groupie like Maddie, are you?"

"Don't be silly, it's just you," she said, taking his hand.

"Well, that's this century's punishment for adultery: the adulterers get stuck with each other - but sometimes it's a reward, a performance bonus for productive sinning!"

"What do you mean, productive?" she asked warily.

"Ah," said Ollie, "I intended to mention precautions last night, but somehow it slipped my mind."

"Don't worry, I'm on the pill," said Charlotte, thinking - typical, bloody irresponsible man!

They walked to the office together, back past the Children's Hospital, holding hands part of the way and making no attempt to conceal their joint arrival.

"Sleep well?" crowed Maddie.

"Mind your own business, you harpy!" Charlotte responded, before thinking better of it and telling her about the Timmy intrusion.

"Have it out with him - don't wait for the axe!" she was advised.

The phone rang. Maddie, as always, answered. She listened, then handed it to Charlotte saying:

"Too late - Sarah says some man wants to talk to you after last night."

Charlotte took the phone and shouted:

"You bastard! How could you? I never thought you'd sink so low!"

Then she listened for a moment and said:

"Oh Graham, I'm terribly sorry! I was expecting someone else."

She covered the receiver and hissed:

"Do be quiet!" fiercely to a guffawing Maddie.

"Yes, yes, yes," she then said into the 'phone, "Of course I'm interested. Whenever suits you. OK next Wednesday it is. I'll be there. Looking forward to it."

"What in God's name was that about?" enquired

Chapter Sixteen

Maddie with customary subtlety.

"Solicitor I used to work for. Met him at the wine-tasting. He's offering me a job. Says he'll double my money!"

At which Maddie began to sing:

"I don't want to lose you but I think you ought to go!"

"An offer I can't refuse?" asked Charlotte. "You're probably right in the circs but first I think I'll take your earlier advice."

She rang Timmy: "What's Arms up to?"

"I suppose you mean Mr Scott," was the reply. "No idea what you're talking about and even if I had my work is guaranteed confidential."

"Oh come on Timmy, for old times' sake," she wheedled.

"All I'm going to say is that you've got the wrong client - I wasn't working for Mr Scott last night."

And having imparted that piece of negative but unexpected information, technically perhaps not in breach of client-confidence, Timothy Lloyd, private detective of discretion, rang off.

Ollie entered without ceremony but with cup.

"No time wasted," he said to Charlotte grimly, ignoring Maddie, and helped himself distractedly to coffee.

"Come and see what I've got."

Charlotte followed him off down the corridor, mouthing to Maddie:

"Tell you later."

The envelope was addressed to Professor Oliver

Goodman and marked 'Strictly Private - For The Ombudsman's Eyes Only'. Miraculously and fortunately, Sarah had, evidently, respected this marking. Inside, Charlotte saw, were two photographs of Ollie and herself *deshabille* cowering in the doorway to his flat. There was also a short cryptic instruction:

'REVERSE CARNWATH OR ELSE'

Underneath in small print was typed: 'details to follow'.

Ollie looked dejectedly at Charlotte: "Do you know what it means, Lot? Because I'm damned if I do - and damned if I don't!"

After a while she found the file.

"My Catch 17 Case," she exclaimed. "A provisional decision in BIG's favour. Remember - death claim under life policy by widow but failed on the ground of non-disclosure of dialysis treatment. Timmy must be working for the punter, Mrs Carnwath!"

"That's certainly a surprise," Ollie opined, frowning. "But there's still the 'or else' to be faced."

Charlotte felt fatalistic, as though Graham's offer had put an irrevocable seal on the previous night's momentous movings.

"She lives in Clapham. That's not far. I'll go and talk to her!"

"Are you sure?" asked Ollie.

"Think of it as pro-active investigation - why should your Assistants be desk-bound?" she replied.

"Don't go by Omnibus," said he, more like himself. "You might meet the legendary man!"

A reasonable woman, she went by Underground.

Chapter Sixteen

Straight through from Holborn to Clapham Common. Half-a mile's walk away, Mrs Carnwath lived in a small, subsiding terraced house in narrow, parked-up Caldervale Road, not handy for shops or the Common itself. She appeared pleased Charlotte was visiting, whoever she was. They sat at a table in the parlour, drinking a nice cup of tea. It was obviously unbelievable straightaway that this elderly lady, of limited means, only recently bereaved and still in mourning, was not up to blackmail. So instead they discussed the provisional decision.

"It was in this very room that he signed up for the policy. He sat there where you're sitting now, I was over there, and Philip sat here where I am," Mrs Carnwath was explaining.

"Who's Philip?" Charlotte interrupted.

"Our nephew, me brother's boy, Philip Otton, he was working for BIG as a salesman then and we were just doing him a favour, buying some life insurance to help him with his career. But he didn't stay with BIG."

"Why didn't you tell him about the dialysis?"

"Oh he knew all about that - could see the machine, couldn't he? It's over there behind you - he said it didn't matter."

Charlotte turned round. Sure enough, there was a kidney dialysis machine, in use as a sideboard but otherwise in full view. Her eyes filled with tears but she asked:

"Where's Philip working now?"

"Estate Agents, opposite the Catholic Church, where the funeral was, down near the Common. He's doing very nicely, so he tells me," said Mrs Carnwath: "But says he can't help me with BIG although he knows I could do with the money. And why isn't the Omnibusman on my side?"

"He didn't know all the facts, but it's not too late to put that right."

Charlotte ignored the 'For Sale' and 'To Let' particulars in the window and entered the 'flats and houses' shop boldly. A wannebe yuppie, on his own, fag and mag, brightened and asked:

"Need any help?"

"I'm looking for a Philip Otton," she said.

"That's me, what can I do you for? Ha ha!"

Not another queer leerer, she thought.

"Well it's to do with your uncle, the late Mr Carnwath. Your Aunt said I'd find you here."

"What about him, then, poor old sod?" said Philip.

"I work for the Insurance Ombudsman and I'm told it was you who sold him his BIG life policy - is that right?"

"Sure, what of it? I sold 'em to all the relatives - everyone does to get going."

"You sold it to him even though you knew he was on dialysis. That's also right, isn't it?" she asked, adding somewhat bluntly: "Not a good risk for BIG, was it?"

"Well I don't know about that," he said. "I was only a trainee but we'd had this bod from head office give a seminar about this brilliant new life policy we were all supposed to flog. Lots of lovely commission! He kept saying: 'ask no questions and you'll be told no lies'. The big idea was get the punter hooked if you thought he'd

Chapter Sixteen

last five years, cause after that they'd not be paying anyway."

"Why wouldn't they be paying? Was it because of Clause 17?"

"Never heard anything about that," he said, "don't remember him saying why they wouldn't be paying - just that that was the way the policy was structured."

"Did you ever have to read the policy?"

"Do me a favour, 'course not! We all sold them to the family and friends as quick as possible and collected the commission. Then we ran out of prospects and with no salary had to move on. I was lucky to find this job, not much different really. Anyway, shame about Uncle Eric, don't understand why BIG's not paying up but it's nothing to do with me now."

"Who was the bod, the one who gave the trainee seminar?" she asked.

"Not sure of his name anymore - something like 'lightening', but some of them called him 'fingers', I remember!"

Charlotte returned to the office and reported to Ollie. However, he too had a development to report: BIG's Bob had telephoned to express his personal concern about the Carnwath provisional. He did not want to influence the decision himself naturally, but since BIG's repudiation was being upheld, surely nothing need be said about Clause 17. In his view, if that part of the decision were to be accepted and applied generally, potentially serious repercussions could be caused for BIG's solvency margins. Nearly 200,000 policies had been sold containing Clause 17, so millions of pounds were at stake. Careful consideration was called for and leading counsel ought to be consulted on the legal position - indeed he would strongly recommend going to Bolsover QC again who could always be relied upon to give a quick, appropriate opinion. In the meantime Ollie would understand that the matter was extremely 'price-sensitive', share values might well be adversely affected so that 'insider-dealing' could occur. Best kept completely confidential.

"Did he threaten anything?" Charlotte asked, beginning to think BIG Bob must have been Timmy's client.

"No, nothing at all, trusted to my sense of responsibility and the fact that BIG proposed increasing the ex gratia payment to Mrs Carnwath to a sum worth having. However, he did say quite a lot about Council's shenanigans yesterday upsetting his confidence in the scheme."

"His premise is wrong now," observed Charlotte thoughtfully. "BIG's repudiation for non-disclosure won't hold water in the light of her nephew's story."

"And telling a Professor of Law to go to a tame barrister for advice might be thought recklessly counter-productive," said Ollie ominously. "Once bitten, twice as extrovert!"

More like a red rag soaked in petrol to a bully in a biscuit factory, Charlotte actually thought, although wondering what she meant.

"So should I redraft the decision, dis-allowing both repudiation and Clause 17?" she asked.

"Reverse Carnwath, you mean, as instructed?"

Chapter Sixteen

replied Ollie. "Yes, you should, no proper alternative, but I suspect we'll still have to face the 'Or Else' anyway.

They repaired to the relative privacy of Stefano's for a late lunch, liquid but not alcoholic.

"We're not talking one-night-stand or *Fatal Attraction* here are we?"

Ollie had asked this, rhetorically on his part Charlotte hoped. She shook her head, fairly sure for her part.

"And it's known to your private eye," - not mine, she thought - "and his client, so we can't expect it to stay secret from our spouses for long. On the contrary, in fact. What do you think we should do, Lot?"

Consulted directly, she sipped reflectively:

"Only two options as I see it. One is to do nothing but cross our fingers" - and legs, she thought - "trusting to fate. But I don't want my fate in hostile hands. The other option is to own up before we're shown up."

"That's what I think too," he said. "The 'do-nothing' option is always deceptively attractive, seems easier at first but tends to make things harder in the long run."

Speaking from previous experience? she speculated.

After very little deliberation, an immediate and, she thought, simplistic plan of action was signed, sealed and delivered, so to speak. They would return to their constituencies and prepare for - at best opposition, she supposed. Ollie was to go home straightaway and he would tell Beryl the truth, possibly the whole truth and perhaps nothing but the truth. Charlotte was likewise to go home there and then and she would tell Simon the truth, likewise edited so as to economise on the aggro. They were to exchange accounts - "Oh and the draft Carnwath decision" - next morning at the office.

If still capable of walking and talking, she thought apprehensively, setting off from Stefano's for Liverpool Street Station and Chelmsford whilst Ollie left for Euston and the North Midlands.

Chapter Seventeen

Friday's Fortune

Reaching the office at a much later hour than ever before, feeling generally relieved and relaxed, Charlotte was very ready to give her account to, she noted, an unwounded but worried Ollie.

"Where've you been 'til this hour, Lot?" he demanded, a touch querulously she thought, as he closed his office door. "I didn't know what to do!"

"You could've drafted the Carnwath decision yourself, I suppose, Ollie darling," she said. "But don't worry, I worked on it last night and there'll be a fair copy on your desk for approval before lunch."

"Not Carnwath, Lot, your spouse! Stop winding me up and tell me what happened."

So she told him.

When she had reached home at a much earlier hour than ever before, not only were the twins still at playschool but slimy Simon was still in bed with Nanny Rosa. After shouting at them for form's sake and ignoring protestations of innocence as similarly for form's sake, she had quickly packed a couple bags while they were left to dress. Then she had taken the Golf, collected the twins and driven to Islington where her mother had welcomed them enthusiastically. Simon had followed later in the evening, without Rosa and after the twins were asleep.

Despite her mother's reluctant reception of her spouse, Charlotte and Simon had managed a civilised discussion of the situation. They no longer spoke for form's sake and so it was a discussion involving full disclosure on each side supported by declarations of serious intentions as to significant others, Rosa and Ollie respectively. A divorce would be arranged, hopefully amicable although financial as well as custodial details were still to be settled. He had departed expressing regret and his intention of instructing a specialist divorce lawyer the next morning, conveniently he had already had recommended to him a practice located in Gray's Inn - he couldn't quite recall the firm's name, but the practitioner himself was apparently known at the rugger club as 'sexy Dick'.

The discussion had taken place in the privacy of the first floor salon, but Charlotte strongly suspected that the room was bugged and that her mother had eavesdropped. In any event, she had soon extracted her daughter's compromising story. Far from being upset, her mother was excited: it emerged that she was actually a fan of Ollie and could hardly wait to meet him. The explanation for this surprising groupie status rested with a neighbour, Adam Kirk.

A successful author of science-fiction stories, Adam had recently moved to Islington and quickly become a friend, a close friend, of Charlotte's mother. Before moving in, he had spent a fortune refurbishing his house, but burglars had removed some of the more valuable refurbishments, such as antique fireplaces and marble statues. BIG had been his insurer but BIG had declined

Chapter Seventeen

payment: BIG's household policy expressly excluded pre-occupation losses - he should have read the small-print. However, Ollie our hero had ordered BIG to pay up: BIG's sales rep had known what Adam was doing and had orally assured him he was covered, therefore the declinature - to re-use insurer-speak - was, in the circumstances, unfair and unreasonable.

Thus Charlotte's illicit relationship with Ollie had, somewhat fortuitously, received her mother's blessing. This was the more so because it had incidentally resulted in the longed-for relocation of her grandchildren. Indeed she had already reorganised two bedrooms to accommodate the three of them and recruited her daily help as a minder. Leaving her mother happily researching local play-schools, Charlotte had driven off to the office, getting trapped in traffic around first the Angel and then King's Cross and thinking there must be better routes. Eventually, however, she found the way round all the one-way systems to the office and parked the Golf nearby in the spiral hole beneath Bloomsbury Square masquerading as a car park, but in reality given the charges undoubtedly a gold-mine.

"So I seem to be blackmail-proof," she concluded her account. "What about you?"

Ollie, unaccustomed as he was to listening, at least for long, appeared distracted.

"I remember the Kirk case," he said. "One of my first - ended the honeymoon period so far as Arms was concerned, he kept twitching his nose and muttering about BIG not being a charitable institution set up to relieve the poverty of the undeserving rich!"

"Come on, you blighter," Charlotte was irritated by at impatient at his apparent distraction. "How did you get on with your spouse?"

"Not too dissimilarly, actually, Lot," he said. "But the peculiar thing was that Kirk wasn't at all grateful - he'd wanted his solicitors' costs as well and I wouldn't make BIG pay them."

Charlotte hit him, not altogether lightly, on the head with the Carnwath file:

"Tell me the tale, Ollie, now - or else!"

"When I turned up a day earlier than expected, Beryl wasn't in bed with anyone but she did try to keep me out of the bedroom. She failed as it happened, not because I was suspicious of anything but because I always change into an old pullover when I get back North."

He paused and Charlotte thought any more digressions and I'll burn the bloody pullover.

"Anyway I discovered straightaway why she'd been trying to keep me out. There were unmistakable signs everywhere not only of bed-sharing but of with whom. I was gob-smacked, I'd had no idea," Ollie added, "Though now with hindsight the clues seem pretty obvious."

"Who was he? How did you know him?" Charlotte asked.

"Not a 'him'," he replied. "It was *Dotty*. Remember my lecture?"

Unforgettable, she thought, in all sorts of ways.

"Her peculiarly distinctive clothing was lying about all over the place. Just as she must have been!"

"Well, we then went downstairs and indulged in a mutual confession session. Beryl'd been a closet lesbian

Chapter Seventeen

all her life, married me for respectability or a cure. Not cured but respectable until Dotty turned up. They found each other out about the time I became Ombudsman and came to London. Brought together because Dotty's first language used to be French. Apparently Dotty visited the Faculty as an external examiner, stayed with Beryl and introduced her to internal examinations as well as advanced French conversation - not her first closet conquest."

"Does her husband know?" asked Charlotte.

"Roy suspects nothing and nobody except me - in fact, I was prepared to blame him for your private eye," said Ollie. "At least I'd have been proved not guilty as charged!"

"So what was the outcome?" Charlotte demanded.

"Not to come out," said Ollie. "Beryl may be incurable but she wants to be thought respectable. As indeed does Dotty. She came back while I was there and after throwing a few hysterics she joined in the discussion. She definitely doesn't want Roy to find her out."

"No divorce then?"

"Lesbianism is not in itself a ground for divorce, unlike adultery, although it would probably be regarded as unreasonable behaviour, unless perhaps we got a female judge!" Ollie said.

"Anyway Beryl made it clear that she wasn't ready to emerge from the closet yet and would like appearances kept up."

"So it's a stand-off - nobody dare blackmail anybody."

"Not exactly," said he. "I don't care anymore about

disclosure to Beryl, nor does she to me, but she cares about disclosure to the world, and so does Dotty, whilst I don't."

"So all in all we feel happily blackmail proof," Charlotte concluded.

"Absolutely, so let's finish off this Carnwath Case!"

Charlotte returned to the Council Chamber so-called, ignoring Sarah and even Marian on the way with ease and Maddie on arrival less easily:

"I'll tell you the whole story later, you bitch, promise, but right now I've got to get this damn decision drafted, so just shut up and let me get on with it!"

After these few well-chosen words, she produced a re-draft which reversed the non-disclosure aspect on the new evidence from Philip Otton, and also confirmed that BIG could not rely on Clause 17 because of failing the Court of Appeal's 'attention test'. In addition, she inserted a passage saying that the law was not entirely clear, but that it was unnecessary to seek advice as to what the law was because the Ombudsman considered that, in all the circumstances of the case, it would not be fair and reasonable for BIG to rely on the small print.

Ollie approved of her re-draft, especially the addition, and was ready to sign it but thought BIG's Bob should be warned of its impending issue. So he rang head office only to be told that that Mr Walker was working from home.

"Where's that?" he had enquired, but naturally the address was not to be revealed over the phone.

"Can I ring him, then?"

But she was not at liberty to reveal the number

Chapter Seventeen

either and, anyway, her instructions were that he did not wish to be disturbed. However, if Professor Goodman cared to leave a message she would see that Mr Walker received it as soon as he arrived on Monday morning.

"Bugger that," said Ollie to Charlotte, "I know where he lives, I've been to his house for festive drinks - East Grinstead, got the address here, but not the telephone number."

It turned out to be ex-directory.

"Sod it," said Ollie. "Only one thing for it, we'll deliver it in person!"

"You mean serve it like a writ?" Charlotte asked resignedly and, after an affirmative answer, enquired: "How will you get there?"

"We'll drive down, right away. Won't take long. You've got your car here, haven't you ?"

Chapter Eighteen

Fatal Friday

En route to East Grinstead, fringe religion capital of the kingdom - or correctly queendom, or even 'dom - with Ollie safely belted into the passenger seat, Charlotte ventured to mention the job offer from Graham. Obviously not too pleased but:

"Not too surprised," said Ollie. "Coincidences abound!"

Apparently Janet Sloss *née* Smith had rung that morning wanting to sound out her dear old Prof on the idea that Oppenheimers should keep up with the Linklaters and the Nabarros of this professional world by appointing a pet academic as their very own Director of Education and Training. If Ollie was at all interested in the idea perhaps they could meet. So a meeting, not something else, would be arranged, not privately but facing her partners.

"Not really keen but I've another iron in the fire - Director of the Institute of Advanced Legal Studies, in Russell Square."

"I know, I know, I've visited, often," said Charlotte.

"Always been a glorified librarian, but now they want both a dynamic leader of research and an effective fund-raiser. I don't fancy either of those rôles much," said Ollie. "Both would be impossible and the pay's pretty poor, but the location would be exceptionally

Chapter Eighteen

convenient, to say nothing of the Director's private accommodation!"

The traffic proved not too bad at mid-day, Brixton was for once not grid-locked and the M23 outside commuter times was virtually vehicle free. With Charlotte not a respecter of speed limits, they reached East Grinstead comfortably in time for lunch - had they been invited. Ollie recalled that BIG's Bob had chosen to live, not only in a town equally inaccessible from each of his places of work, in London and in Bournemouth respectively, but also on an estate of individual, maturer executives' houses, all with extensive enough gardens for them to feel like country landowners.

"Bonewood," he said. "Private road, turn right just before the Grand Temple of the Latter Day Saints, no number - the house is called *Fox's Folly*, up the hillock on the left."

She parked as he instructed, across the road and just past the house.

The wide winding drive to a double garage beside a big bungaloid, not to say huge hut-like, residence was blocked by a red BMW.

"That's Bob's car, a BIG perk for the MD," said Ollie. "Looks like he's at home."

Not to us perhaps, thought Charlotte, asking: "Are we both visiting?"

"Better be me," said her hero. "He doesn't know you and might jump to conclusions."

"What conclusions?"

"Oh press or police - blackmail is criminal after all.

You wait and watch - if I'm not out in an hour, send in a search party!"

Ollie took the Carnwath file with the finalised draft decision, squeezed beside the BMW and rang an antique-style doorbell. Curtains twitched at the side of a square-bayed window, a woman's face it seemed to Charlotte. Then after a pause the door was opened and filled by BIG's Bob himself. Ollie spoke shortly but, judging by his free hand's gestures, pointedly. Bob stood aside slowly and his Ombudsman entered quickly as the door slammed shut.

Charlotte's waiting and watching, via an adjusted rear-view mirror, remained entirely uneventful for twenty minutes. Then she heard another car. A taxi stopped outside *Fox's Folly* and Fingers emerged. The taxi departed and he was let in without difficulty or delay, as if expected. She wondered what was going on and worried a bit, recalling not only Philip Otton's account of the 'bloke' promoting the policies containing Clause 17 but also the Finance Director's apparent aspirations to succeed BIG's Bob as MD.

After another twenty minutes she worried a lot. A loud explosion occurred at the back of the house and Fingers erupted through the front door. He hurried to the BMW, peered in, got in, started up, reversed out and drove off fast down the hillock.

No other sound or sign of life came from the house but a spiral of smoke grew and thickened at the back. Charlotte ran from the car to ring the doorbell. Nothing happened for long moments. Unable to wait she ran on round the side of the house to the back. Another

CHAPTER EIGHTEEN

door into a smoke-filled room - locked. On to the next - a window. Through this she saw no smoke but Ollie, alone, in a wide armchair apparently perusing an ancient parchment! She banged on the window. He turned around, saw her with undisguised surprise, looked at his watch, then opened the window.

"What's the matter? Is the hour up?" he asked.

"No you idiot, didn't you hear the bang? The house is on fire, get out through the window. Fingers has escaped but where's Bob?"

"He was getting us some coffee, left me with his title deeds, needs advice on a boundary dispute," said Ollie, beginning to climb out without agility but with some urgency.

At that moment the door to the room opened and Bob staggered in, dishevelled clothes and black-faced.

"Sorry about the coffee," he said. "A technical hitch in the kitchen but I've extinguished the flames. Hey! Where are you going and who's that young woman? Are you eloping?"

Ollie reversed clumsily into the room, pulling Charlotte in after him.

"May I introduce my Legal Assistant, Ms Angus - Mr Robert Walker - she's been helping me on the Carnwath case."

BIG's Bob shook hands, saying:

"I've heard of you - from Scottie, doesn't - ah - always agree with you, I gather."

Then through the door came a woman's cry of distress:

"Bob, where are you? Are you alright? Why is there

smoke everywhere? I've dialled 999, fire brigade's on its way!"

Lady Cocks entered wearing a capacious bathrobe, boldly and goldly initialled RW, her head - with or without wig - turbaned in a towel. She wore embarrassment too when she saw who was there.

"We've still got visitors, our Jenny," said Bob, "You'll have met them already."

By all that's wonderful - up to no good together! marvelled Charlotte.

"I thought everyone had left with Mr Lightman in the BMW. I saw him drive off."

"In the BMW?" bellowed Bob, "That's mine!"

"You must have left the keys in the ignition," Charlotte dared to say.

"Of course I did, perfectly safe on this estate - no riff raff, except the religious loonies, of course, and they don't pinch cars!"

"But was Mr Lightman responsible for the explosion and what is he up to now?" Charlotte enquired urgently. "Surely the police should be notified."

However, they decided the explosion was an accident: Lady Cocks had just put a leg of lamb in the oven when Ollie rang the doorbell. Seeing who was at the door, she had hidden in the bedroom, forgetting to light the gas. Bob's attempt to produce coffee had been the proximate cause of the explosion.

Lack of reasonable care, thought Charlotte, but would any insurer dare decline?

"The last thing Lightman said," remembered Bob, "was that if the widow Carnworth couldn't be bought

CHAPTER EIGHTEEN

off, he'd still get her to withdraw her claim somehow so as to stop you issuing the decision."

"It's especially important to Mr Lightman, is it?" asked Charlotte.

"Certainly is," replied Bob. "His whole future's on the line. That Clause 17 device was all his idea - sort of disguised term insurance, short-term life cover instead of whole life. It was going to bring profitability to our life business and put him up with Weinberg in industry estimation. It's proved profitable alright, we've sold nearly 200,000 of these policies. But if we have to carry on carrying maximum cover for minimal premiums we'll go bust."

"Is that why you set a private eye onto me and sank to blackmail?" demanded Ollie.

Bob looked bewildered. Plainly none of the skulduggery had anything to do with him: it was obviously the first he had heard of it.

"So Timmy's client, the blackmailer, must be Fingers," cried Charlotte. "What else is he capable of? He's on his way to deal with old Mrs Carnwath right now. We should get round there as quickly as possible to stop him - he might resort to violence!"

With that dramatic excuse, declining a purely polite late-luncheon invitation - cold leftovers, of course - and accepting belated assurances of the innocence of Lady Cocks's presence - necessary discussions as to Council's chairmanship and the scheme's constitution, plus a few family matters - Ollie and Charlotte left to chase Fingers. They did not chase far. Having turned the Golf so as to speed off the Bonewood estate, suddenly the hillock was alive with the sound of sirens.

"That'll be naughty Cocksey's fire engines," observed Ollie.

He was wrong. True there was a fire-engine, but the sirens were from police cars and an ambulance. BIG's Bob's red BMW had crashed at the junction head-on into the big red fire-engine and, they could see, come off very much worse.

Chapter Nineteen

Weekend Break

Fingers had been cut, still conscious, from the wreckage by fire-fighters, and stretchered-off by ambulancemen. During his ordeal he had been comforted in turn by the variously dressed representatives of a variety of religious organisations. When materialistic assistance had arrived, they had dispersed to watch and pray, some of them aloud and tunefully. Whatever his spiritual condition or state of mind after this, Fingers' physical injuries demanded that he be driven away immediately to the intensive care unit of the emergency hospital near Gatwick Airport.

Ollie and Charlotte having watched with helpless and horrified curiosity returned to *Fox's Folly* to break the bad news to BIG's Bob. They now found him dressing-gowned, with 'our Jenny', handbag hidden, no longer bath-robed and, instead of the towel turban on her head, she was again purplishly bewigged, except that it appeared to be untidily like otherwise ordinary hair. Charlotte felt sure that BIG's Bob might, in all the circumstances, have felt reluctant to tempt fate by encouraging the blackmailing of other adulterers: he was a widower, she knew, but Lord Cocks's obituary had yet to be published. That elderly and infirm peer was exceptionally wealthy and whilst revelations might hasten his demise and so obviate divorce proceedings they might not do so before he could alter his will. His Jenny would be at risk financially, she reasoned.

They were all inordinately distressed as well as disturbed. It was agreed that serious and significant decisions would have to be reached about the future - of the scheme, of BIG itself and indeed of the four of them, as individuals both privately and publicly. Such decisions should, however, be allowed to brew if not ferment over the week-end.

At that profoundly sensitive point, they heard another car arrive. The door bell rang but before BIG's Bob could budge, it was opened and closed. A handsome woman of forty or thereabouts dressed in casual tweeds strode into the room where they were still sitting.

"Joanna!" cried Lady Cocks, rising dramatically. "Thought it might be you - terrible things have been happening!"

"What things, Mummy?" cried Joanna back. "Alex at the club said there'd been a fire and a crash. Are you both alright? Bob darling what's going on? Who are these people?"

She looked angry but at home.

"Everything's under control Jo," said BIG's Bob standing now and embracing the new arrival. "No damage here worth mentioning - except to your mother's lamb, we'll have to have a cold lunch today."

He turned to the open-mouthed Ollie and the wide-eyed Charlotte:

"Let me introduce my wife, Joanna, Lady Cocks' daughter - Jo this is my Ombudsman, Professor Goodman, and his assistant, Ms Angus. Called on an

Chapter Nineteen

urgent case, but they're just leaving."

Magisterial in his dressing-gown, he escorted them back to the Golf, past Joanna's two-seater Mercedes, explaining that his re-marriage was not yet public knowledge:

"Not been a widower long, known Joanna Cocks for some years - golf, you know - but not closely, of course, marriage was an unexpected development. Register office, short notice, last month - church blessing and announcements later this month, keep it quiet until then, eh?"

Charlotte drove with uncharacteristic, speed-abiding caution back towards London. Whether this was because of Fingers' accident or because of guilt at mentally maligning Lady Cocks and BIG's Bob, she could not be sure. Her chosen route would be via Clapham, but re-visiting Mrs Carnwath appeared inappropriate. Just outside East Grinstead they had stopped for a belated pub lunch; Ollie consumed a ploughman's and a pint while she nibbled a smoked salmon sandwich and sipped a Perrier. At length she dropped Ollie outside Trinity Court. During the drive and at the pub they talked little about the day's events and less about the long-term future, although he did address the short-term, suggesting she stay the night at his flat. However the suggestion lacked conviction, partly because no overnight bag had been packed in anticipation but mainly because the twins might expect their mother to put in an appearance. So she declined, reluctantly since they still needed to talk - if not to sleep - together, and assured him she would be in touch that evening about getting together that weekend.

True to her word, Charlotte telephoned Ollie later and they did get together. He accepted her mother's invitation to dine in Islington on the Saturday evening. Adam Kirk was also there and dominated the conversation, concentrating on authors' problems with publishers to the virtual exclusion of various interesting aspects of insurance law and practice which Ollie might have mentioned. Adam did refer briefly to his own claim, upheld by Ollie, with gratitude and not complaining of employing a solicitor but about the expenditure of his own time which he considered chargeable at the same hourly rate. Charlotte noticed that, although her Ombudsman soon sank into silence, evidently dissatisfied with the conversation, his satisfaction with the wine was constituting more than adequate compensation. Eventually she sent him back to Trinity Court in a taxi, before he disgraced himself, confident that the driver would know its whereabouts thanks to *Mona Lisa.*

On Sunday morning she took Ollie, and her terrible twins, to London Zoo. It was wet and windy but Danny and Benjy loved the elephants performing, particularly urinating, so much so that they abandoned sibling warfare and stood waiting and watching, passively patient in the rain. They were lured away for lunch after an interminable hour or two, tempted by the restaurant - a Chinese junk moored in Regent's Canal. There, however, they ended their pacifist truce. Far from a tranquil tête-à-tête repast, thought Charlotte, despite putting on a good face, Ollie will not be pleased.

CHAPTER NINETEEN

Afternoon tea with mother. No Adam, but twins emulating elephants at play, encouraged tolerantly by their grandmother until she realised the lavatorial nature of their activities when they were hastily handed over to Charlotte's control. Ollie recalled childhood visits to the Zoo. His father had been not only an atheist but also a Member of the Royal Zoological Society. The former excluded church attendance whilst the latter included free entrance on Sunday mornings, so little Ollie and his littler sister, Jessie, were taken religiously each week, for years and years it seemed to him, consoled not by Chinese-junk meals but by ice-creams.

"In those days," he told the twins, still acting, as he had tried to all day thought Charlotte, his 'Ollie the jolly uncle' role, "Children like you could have sixpenny rides in a fancy carriage on top of a huge old elephant - you'd have loved it, but Jessie was always terrified, and I wasn't much better. I'm not sure why they stopped the rides, safety regulations or perhaps the insurance premiums were too high!"

The twins merely regarded him gravely and asked: "What's Daddy doing?" and "Where do you live?"

Charlotte drove Ollie back to Trinity Court. Sitting outside in the Golf, he wondered aloud when, or rather whether, she would stay and be his love again. She not only recognised his new 'abandoned lover' role, with added pathos in reserve, but had anticipated it.

"This Wednesday," she said decisively. "If you're free - and can wait that long! I've already warned my mother and there's no problem at my end."

He laughed, putting pathos away for later:

"A week to the day, Lot! No Council meeting, no wine-tasting - at least not with other solicitors - no private-eye with any luck. What will we have to talk about?"

"As Anthony said to Cleopatra, on entering her tent, 'I've not come here to talk!'" she replied. "Heard a distinguished after-dinner speaker begin by saying that when I was a student. He then said: 'But I'll give my address anyway - it's number five, Stone Court, and I'm going there now' and he left! A retired judge, past his bed-time."

"Bet the students didn't mind at all," said Ollie. "Meant they could get down to serious drinking sooner."

"Actually it was their serious drinking which had delayed the dinner and upset his lordship. However, we shouldn't be short of something to talk about. A great deal's happened since last week, but won't more have to happen in the next day or two?"

"Probably," he said sighing. "Decisions, decisions! - Issue Carnwath determination? Inform police about Fingers' blackmail? Resign as Ombudsman? God knows what BIG's Bob will do!"

"Well I'm seeing Graham on Wednesday, lunchtime, to discuss his job offer, he thinks, but I'm also thinking of taking his advice about the divorce from Simon. In the meantime we'd both better sleep on everything - separately," she added hastily.

Without protest, he kissed her cheek, got out and waved her off.

Chapter Twenty

Engagement Day

Monday morning, well-advised by a neighbour admiring the twins, Charlotte left the Golf parked in her mother's street and took the tube, standing squeezed amongst strangers, the Victoria line from Highbury & Islington to Euston and a short walk down Southampton Row to the office. Apart from the other passengers, their quantity not their quality, it was quite a convenient journey, she thought, not only for the office but for Ollie's flat too.

Sarah smiled at her - shyly? Surely not! Was something up? She was not on the telephone! Charlotte felt apprehensive.

Maddie greeted her loudly:

"Where did you get to with the Prof on Friday, Lottie? Up to no good again, I know! Never mind, did she tell you her news? Do you believe it?"

"Quieten down, you hussy, you're worse than the twins. What news are you talking about?"

"I think it's just a joke - Sarah says she's engaged to Marian and they're getting married on Friday, registry office in Kensington!"

"What did you say?"

"I laughed in her face, said 'very funny, Friday the thirteenth, unlucky for some - and everyone knows he's gay!'" Maddie began to sound less loud.

"And what did she say to that?" asked Charlotte remembering last Wednesday spotting hand-holding after the Council meeting as well as that morning's shy smile.

"She just said 'Not everyone' and flounced out. I went to see if Marian knew but he was in with the Prof - doors closed. She'd already told Chip and Mount and they were still swapping obscenities, but I found old Hard-on crying!"

Charlotte dumped her bag and dashed out to reception:

"Sarah, is it true? You and Robin? Getting married?"

A shy nod.

"Congratulations! Congratulations! Let me hug you!"

The receptionist received kisses on the cheeks as well as a hug with a big smile and said:

"Stop crying Lottie, it's nothing to cry about!"

"Can't help it," wept Charlotte. "Back in a minute."

She hurried out of the office, down the stairs and out of the building. From the gift shop in Sicilian Avenue she bought a big box of Belgian chocolates, a bottle of Champagne and a congratulatory card.

Having smuggled her purchases past Sarah in a large plastic bag and with a tearful smile, she closed the Council Chamber door firmly behind her.

"Come on Maddie, she was telling the truth - let's hope it's not too late to put it right. Sign this card with me and we'll give them these jointly. And don't call him Marian ever again!"

For once Maddie did as Charlotte told her without a

CHAPTER TWENTY

shout. They emerged into the corridor as Sarah's fiancé, no longer to be known as Marian, emerged at the other end from Ollie's room - cheeks flushed?

"Master Manager Sir and Missy Sarah, Ma'am to be," Maddie had retrieved her tongue, Charlotte worried what she'd say, "We on your staff were overwhelmed as well as thrilled by your unexpected tidings. Please to accept our sincerest congratulations together with these tokens of our appreciation, borne by my colleague here, little lawyer Lottie."

And Maddie actually threw her arms round her former antagonist, said:

"Well done, Robin," and kissed him without any evident reservations.

The Manager surfaced, not offended, no leer, still surprise mixed with pleasure. Sarah smiled at him with relief - and love? Maddie kissed her too, with restraint if not reservations, whilst Charlotte dripped tears on Robin.

Back in their Council Chamber, Maddie wailed:

"Wow, did I get that wrong! Lottie, what would I do without you? Saved the day! You're wonderful! Phew, but his moustache ain't a nice tickle!"

"Perhaps you'd better warn Chip and Mount quickly before it's too late to make amends," said Charlotte, feeling she'd done her bit and needing to wash a tear-stained face.

"Right you are, no sooner said than done," yelled Maddie departing as Ollie entered, carrying an empty cup.

"What's up Lot?" he asked with quick concern at her

tear-stained appearance.

"It's only Robin and Sarah, made me all emotional, couldn't help crying. They've told you?"

"Yes, the office-boy. . ."

"Don't call him that anymore!"

". . . Robin came in, closed the door, sat down and said he had something serious to tell me. He wasn't smiling and I thought 'Oh no, not another disaster!' But what he said, very seriously, was that Sarah had moved in with him and they were going to get married."

"You must have been astonished, the girls undoubtedly were," said Charlotte, lapsing from the politically correct, "What did you say?"

"I was absolutely stunned, but he's no joker and I believed him. Wondered for a moment whether she was pregnant - and by whom! Actually said: 'Is it congratulations or commiserations?' Then said, forcing a smile, that traditionally it's commiserations for the bride and congratulations for the groom. At that, thank God, he smiled. So I shook him by the hand and started to ask embarrassing questions. They've been an item for yonks, whatever they may be, the YMCA was only a cover for his mother - and he didn't want Cocksey to know, would undermine his authority as Manager. Doesn't seem to be gay after all!"

"He certainly kept his lengthy licit liaison secret more successfully than we managed with our short illicit one," observed Charlotte, not thinking of Lady Cocks' Joanna and BIG's Bob. "You'd better start camping it up ready for next time."

"I'm not thinking 'short' or 'next time'," Ollie

CHAPTER TWENTY

muttered crossly.

"Nor am I," said Charlotte, not displeased with her quasi-tease. "But I'm going to re-do my face now. Help yourself to coffee and think about breaking the serious news to the office."

So Ollie made the great sacrifice of cancelling his Monday game of bridge and took all of them out to lunch at Stefano's, not simply drinks and snacks at the bar but in the restaurant, ostensibly to celebrate the surprise engagement. With grand gestures, he ordered Champagne all-round and when it had been poured - and Mrs Arden's protests overridden - proposed a toast to the "unexpected couple". Before he could elaborate with his customary wit and tact, Maddie sprang to her feet shouting: "Her, Her" and "Him, Him" and they all drank and congratulated vociferously. The other tables were occupied by a party of Japanese tourists who watched them throughout, flashing the occasional camera, in a way which led Charlotte to think of the Zoo.

Robin responded to Ollie's half-hypocritical toast by inviting them all to their wedding and afterwards at his flat - except Chip and Mount who had so far failed to show sufficient contrition to be forgiven for greeting Sarah's happy announcement with vulgar hilarity. Chip and Mount chortled. Friday the thirteenth was laughed off as lucky for himself and his bride: they could only get married then because the registrar had not been fully booked for superstitious reasons. However, Robin added, their two families would not have met before the big day and he'd be grateful if his colleagues could mingle in a meaningful way, minimising embarrassments and forestalling any outbreak of hostilities - so on second thoughts they would both be delighted if Mount could come too and she might as well bring Chip with her.

He has a sense of humour after all, thought Charlotte, but she had yet to meet either of the two families.

"Have you thought of inviting the Chairman?" Ollie asked.

"If you mean Frankie Freeman, the answer's no," Robin replied vehemently. "But I did wonder about Lady Cocks, we used to see eye to eye on Scheme and Council affairs."

"Sorry, I meant Cocksey," said Ollie. "BIG's Bob phoned this morning - Sarah might have mentioned it to you but as it happened Mrs Arden answered. He advised me that there are plans afoot to consolidate BIG's complaints arrangements into an industry-wide Ombudsman operation involving regulation of all financial services. As a result the new Chair's tenure will regrettably have to be of restricted. . ."

"Growth!" shouted Maddie.

". . . significance," Ollie continued. "So, if I may, my suggestion would be to invite both Bob and his Jenny - bread upon the water, you know."

"Bread and water?" said Mount to Chip.

"To minimise hostilities, no doubt," said Chip to Mount, adding to Sarah: "Where will you go for the honeymoon? We went to Blackpool - that was a lovely afternoon!"

"It's also a line from *The Entertainer*, you tiny toad,"

Chapter Twenty

said Mount, "I know you went to Tenerife, you've told me often enough. Now Sarah to be serious for a second, you should be considering your financial future and providing for children's needs. If you like I'll get my hubby to give you a ring - he'd happily give you good advice."

"That's very kind of you," Sarah began,

"But we'll let you know," Robin concluded.

Ollie then spoilt the fun by giving them a slim version of the previous Friday's events, the truth but definitely not the whole truth. It was edited to protect the genuinely guilty, himself, his Lot and incidentally the blackmailing Fingers, as well as the misjudged guilty, Lady Cocks with BIG's Bob, although hinting misleadingly at marital developments to be announced soon. Charlotte doubted whether his editing could deceive anyone for long, particularly given that she had already told the whole story to Maddie.

Ollie went on to explain that he had signed and issued the redrafted Carnwath determination - already posted by Mrs Arden to the lucky widow and to BIG's head-office in Bournemouth. There it would not be received by Fingers, perhaps fortunately since the Hospital had reported that his condition was still unstable, not just physically but also, in the light of his weird chanting, mentally. Big Bob Walker would certainly see and disapprove the determination, but he would not be taken by surprise and, for personal reasons, was not expected to react vindictively against the scheme. Ollie neglected to mention, however, that he was seriously contemplating deserting the scheme, as if a sinking ship.

Not much more work was done that Monday afternoon. Charlotte herself returned early to Islington to see how the twins were coping with their new play-school - or *vice versa*. All she said to Ollie was: "See you to-morrow morning." He looked a little peeved but only replied: "Hope so."

Tuesday morning Charlotte arrived early at Trinity Court. Ollie's surprise seemed amplified by the entryphone.

"You got me out of the shower," he shouted, as a matter of fact rather than a cause for complaint, "Come up at once, Lot, and I'll punish you with breakfast!"

As before, breakfast consisted of coffee and juice, with apples and cheese, but healthily supplemented by halves of grapefruit and unroasted cashew nuts. Ollie, still in a bath-robe, gave her his spare keys, saying:

"Other people seem to have no problem getting into the building - they just wait for someone else coming in or out, or perhaps ring bells at random until someone unlocks the front door - I told you that's how your private eye gained access."

Not mine, she thought of saying but then thought what's the point?

They reached the office not so late that explanations might be expected, even by Maddie, and the working day, at least, proved comparatively uneventful. Everyone was still full of embarrassed sweetness and smiles, politeness twisted conversation away from its customary frankness. People appeared to concentrate on their work without distracting their colleagues.

Chapter Twenty

Charlotte again left early for the sake of the twins saying:

"See you to-morrow!" to everyone, including Ollie, whilst thinking about troughs between the waves.

Chapter Twenty-One

Last Straw Day

Wednesday morning Charlotte arrived even earlier at Trinity Court, carrying a bag packed for more than one overnight. She let herself into the building, rode the front open-to-view lift to the sixth floor, quietly opened the door to flat No.69 and peered into the bedroom. Ollie still slept spread-eagled on his back, an early-morning erection evident enough to anyone looking. Charlotte put her bag down and watched him for a while wondering who or what he dreamt of. Then she undressed, slid under the duvet and on top of him. Ollie's arms came round her and pulled her close with such an absence of startled surprise that she doubted that he could really have been sleeping at all. But he was undoubtedly making her welcome.

Later Ollie brought her coffee in bed together with a terribly juvenile joke about the four Ss - something to do shitting, shaving, showering and shagging, but not necessarily in that order. Over breakfast they talked about prospects. Charlotte was to lunch with Graham Lawrence and his attractive job offer. Whilst Ollie half expected to hear somewhat similarly from Janet Sloss and had his other eggs on the boil as well. He had also heard rumours of a number of new Ombudsmen offices being established by Parliament in the next session: one for complaints about solicitors and barristers - "Only

Chapter Twenty-One

open to non-lawyers" - one for complaints about pensions - "Sounds bloody boring!" - and the one for conveyancing - "Should be right up my street." They agreed that he ought to stick it out with the BIG scheme for as long as he could to see what was cooking.

After bedding and breakfasting, they reached the office late enough for explanations, especially to Maddie. However on the day these seemed to be more especially expected by Frances Freeman, Chair of Council, who emerged from Robin the Clerk/Manager's room as they entered the office. She was accompanied not only by a flustered Robin but by a conciliatory youngman.

Ollie, ignoring them all, said: "Good-morning Sarah - any phone calls for me?"

"Yes Prof," replied the receptionist. "Some lady solicitor rang about a lunch date. Wouldn't tell me what for - personal apparently. I said you'd ring back and left a note of her number on your desk."

"Thank you Sarah, of course in America all the solicitors are ladies, ha ha - that's what they call prostitutes, you know Frankie," Ollie explained to that angry looking little woman. "But what on earth are you doing here? Council's not meeting to-day is it?"

"I've come, as Chair of Council, to explore the future of this Ombud-scheme."

Her customary flaring of nostrils and squaring of shoulders were accompanied by a rolling of eyes often signifying, Charlotte thought, at least in school-girls, the recital of a memorised text.

"This is Dick Buxton, special lecturer in sociological-business studies at the South Bank Polytechnic. He's kindly accepted a commission from me on behalf of Council to undertake a research project into the scheme's existing constitution and the office's present operation in order to propose appropriate structural changes to enhance your efficiency and improve your productivity. I was disappointed that you were not here when we arrived - and you know it's now Frances," she concluded focusing fiercely on Ollie, whilst her special lecturer exuded the superior air of an appointed expert.

"But ma Chair Frances," he responded, ignoring the lecturer but fudging a foreign accent and attempting funny Frenchman gestures - she's not amused, observed Charlotte. "Vat iz vrong wiz our, 'ow you say, productivity? My ladees, zey do zer ver best - zer is no backlog just a stockpile of work, no idle hands here!"

"I think it sad that you always defend your Assistants and worse still when you descend to flippancy. This is an aspect of your performance that the Vice-Chair and I will have to address during your re-appointment appraisal - scheduled for next Wednesday," she smiled as if playing a trump.

"Well to be serious and also brutally frank," said Ollie no longer attempting to amuse, "Neither you nor Poly Dickie here are qualified to tell us what to do - nothing against either of you personally, of course, not yet anyway, it's just a little matter of completely lacking any relevant expertise or experience."

"Oh you're being impertinent and dismissive," said the Chair, through her nose, "I'm leaving before I lose my temper!"

Chapter Twenty-One

At which she swept out, nose up, patently in a temper, her researcher trotting uncomfortably after.

Without another word Ollie stumped away down the corridor to his room and slammed the door shut. Charlotte, left in reception, looked at Sarah and Robin, both aghast, raised her eyebrows, said nothing and went off to the Council Chamber. She found Maddie at the door, an obvious eavesdropper.

"What was that all about?"

"Battling for territory," said Charlotte. "But it won't be a war of attrition - I think they've both gone too far already."

"She was in here earlier," said Maddie. "Had Robin take down Cocksie's picture - look what's there now."

Charlotte looked and saw a large photo of the blessed Borrie, proactive Director General of Fair Trading. She said:

"We must be careful not to be caught in the cross-fire!"

"Well look what you've got, a consolation prize."

And Maddie pointed to a bottle of brandy with a thank you note from Mrs Carnwath.

"Lucky nurses or should it be kept, in the circs, for medicinal purposes?"

Ollie's coffee cup entered with him closely attached and waving a piece of paper.

"Look at this cutting," he shouted, "Trust BIG's Bob to have an escape route!"

Charlotte read the headline: 'BIG Merger Talks With Co-operative Insurance'.

"What does it mean?" she asked.

"He's getting out while the going is good - before the implications of our Carnwath determination sink in, or rather sink BIG!"

"He's not going to get away Scott-free," said Maddie. "I had Arms on the phone earlier about a 'joy-riding' claim and he said he wasn't going to pay for the damage to Bob's BMW - lack of reasonable care leaving the key in the ignition and driver other than policyholder not covered for accidents!"

"Does Fingers have one of BIG's medical health policies?" wondered Charlotte, "I bet Arms won't want to pay up on that either."

"And if he dies," crowed Maddie "Arms will say it was suicide, outwith their cover on grounds of public policy!"

She bounced out to tell Chip and Mount.

"Could BIG's Bob complain to us?" asked Charlotte.

"Not after a merger with the Co-op," said Ollie. "They don't believe in Ombudsmen - they're one of the PIAS companies."

"Pious! Does any insurer class itself as pious?"

"Oh they all do, at least in the self-justifying sense. But I was referring to our rival, the Personal Insurance Arbitration Service where disputed claims are submitted to someone selected from a panel of arbitrators."

"Is that popular?"

"Not with consumerists but it is with insurers, despite occasional inconsistencies, so in the long run it or something similar will probably prevail. The arbitrator's decision doesn't involve any investigation

Chapter Twenty-One

by him and doesn't depend on his view of what's fair and reasonable. What's more, it binds the policyholder too, whereas with us, in theory although never - or hardly ever - in reality, a losing punter can have another punt in court."

"So PIAS is not only adversarial and inequitable but also avoids double jeopardy - any solicitor worth his pittance would unhesitatingly advise insurer-clients to prefer it to an Ombudsman scheme like ours," Charlotte observed. "I'm sure I would. In fact there must be potential liability for professional negligence if any lawyer fails to tell an insurer to avoid us like the plague."

"Absolutely, although the attitude of his professional indemnity insurer might be interesting," Ollie replied. "Anyway I happen to know that the Co-op's MD sees BIG's Bob as Dr Frankenstein and me as his monster running amok - they hosted a fancy dress party at one insurance brokers' conference with a 'horror-story' theme: I was invited to 'come as you are'!"

"Did you?"

"No - went to bed with a good bottle, no bad woman being available."

"Who was the phone call from?" Charlotte asked not quite inconsequentially, remembering and worrying a little about what Sarah had said when they arrived.

"Janet Sloss - suggested a pre-partners' interview meeting-lunch, if you see what I mean, we're meeting at Chez Gerrard in Chancery Lane, timely I hope," replied Ollie, "Where are you going with your Graham Lawrence?"

Charlotte laughed: "Snap - I'll be able to keep an eye on you!"

As it turned out they were seated far enough apart in the fashionable basement restaurant to disregard each other discreetly, although Charlotte equally discreetly watched Ollie being winsome with his former student and prospective employer. However she was mostly distracted from watching by the attentions and intentions of her former and future - he hoped - employer. Whilst he had always been like that with women as to personal relations, all bluff she had once discovered - dedicated to his wife, as to employment he was not bluffing and made her an offer she certainly did not think she could refuse. She told him she would probably accept but said she would like to think it over for a couple of days, meaning talk it over with Ollie later.

After lunch, leaving a scowling Ollie unacknowledged, Charlotte was taken by Graham back to his office primarily to view the plush facilities, especially his computerisation projects, and to meet the more presentable of her possible colleagues, but also to give instructions to the firm's divorce specialist. She returned to the Ombudsman's office just in time to join Ollie and the others as they set off for their customary early evening drinks.

Later at Stefano's, after Chip and Mount had gone home and Maddie had left to meet her current 'grey' gentleman, Ollie enquired what Charlotte had had for lunch.

"Steak - rare - salad, mineral water and a very

acceptable job offer. What about you?"

"The same, except my steak was *bien cuit* - I ordered *brulé* but the waiter said the chef would be upset - with *frites* and a glass or two of Beaujolais but not exactly any job offer although Janet seems confident that she's got it fixed if I want it."

"So how does the future feel now?" she asked.

"The prospect of annual appraisal by a scheming schoolgirl was the last intolerable straw," he replied glumly. "Would have been bad enough with a bossy headmistress but at least Cocksey didn't see the chairmanship as her personal stepping stone to fame and fortune. She was already listed as great and good. After the Council coup, so far as concerns the scheme's future, the writing was on the carpet, in blood and tears! So it's time to jump before I'm jettisoned or the scheme's wrecked. Don't really fancy taking on Janet's training wallah role, even assuming her partners agree, but it would be well enough paid and she's brandished prospects of moving on to fee-earning work which might lead to a partnership. Not sure how far she can be trusted but I've definitely decided to abandon Ombudsmanning, at least for the time being, and take my chances answering the call of the wild!"

"When will you do the dirty deed?"

"Friday, I'll give notice with immediate effect - the scheme rules provide for this to happen, by mistake no doubt. What about you?"

"I'll do the same then, accept Graham's job and give notice," she said, "So we can ride off into the Sunset together - holding hands 'cause children's shoes have far to go!"

"I remember that advert," said Ollie, "And it's Sunset now. Come on Lot, I'll buy you the best fish and chips in London, on the way back to the flat."

"Gosh Boss, you certainly know how to show a girl a good time!"

He led her down Southampton Row, then behind the baroque Russell Hotel and beside the barrack-like Brunswick Centre to the North Sea Fisheries in Leigh Street. Next to a traditional chippie take-away was a homely fish restaurant, dominated by a bar, all run briskly by very nearly friendly Italian ladies of uncertain age. The house white by the litre was a quaffable Soave - according to a quaffing Ollie. He ordered grilled skate, boiled potatoes and a wallie - a little pickled cucumber - for himself and plaice in matzo-meal batter and chips - definitely not *frites* - plus peas, not mushy, for Charlotte. The waitress treated him as a regular with tolerant contempt. For dessert - pudding - they shared apple and banana fritters with 'home-made' ice-cream. Everything was completely delicious.

"On Fridays booking's essential - packed out by local Catholics," said Ollie. "Otherwise it's always busy, mostly thanks to American tourists staying at the Russell who think, rightly, that they're experiencing the cuisine of the country and eating with the natives."

Later Charlotte was leading him, a merry staggering gentleman, through Regent Square towards Trinity Court and the dubious sanctuary of his flat. There, as explicitly promised, claret and cheese awaited them. Implicitly promised, she reflected, had been sexual

Chapter Twenty-One

shenanigans:

"Wine's full of living orgasms, you know," he had told her more than once.

But delivery of the shenanigans seemed less and less sure : the wine might be willing but the flesh was full.

Eventually, following a fruitless attempt or two at mad passionate love, Ollie fell asleep with his head on her bottom. She rolled him off, he murmured dopily without waking, she pulled up the duvet and, although it was not late, also slept. . . for a while. Then she lay awake for a while in the moonlight, before trying a trick picked up from slimy Simon: she took the slumbering Ollie's left nipple between her thumb and forefinger and squeezed, harder and harder. The effect proved electric - she conjured an image of Frankenstein creating his monster. Ollie reacted as if galvanised into life: his love-making struck like lightning as he overwhelmed her with violent and prolonged passion - rough hands all around her body, fingers and tongue in mouth, cunt and arse-hole, she was turned over and back and entered and fucked. At last they came convulsively together and she screamed and screamed again, deep in the extremes of orgasm.

"Shush, my Lot, you'll frighten the neighbours," whispered Ollie. "They'll be calling the police. What time is it?" He looked: "My God, only four o'clock!"

They lay side by side, hands grasped, panting and sweating for long satisfyingly exhausted minutes. Then he, in his turn, pulled up the duvet. Holding each other tightly, cheeks touching, they slept once more. . . for a while. She awoke with fierce pins and needles and a raging thirst. Pushed away, Ollie sat up groaning. He looked at her as if amazed and she asked:

"Who am I?"

"You're you," he said, after a pause.

"Not bad, in the circumstances," she said. "Get me a drink of water - sparkling if possible."

"No greater love hath any man than that he gets up in the night to bring a drink for his friend," grumbled Ollie, obeying.

"That wasn't all you got up for."

Chapter Twenty-Two

Penultimate Morning

Next morning they overslept but woke tired. Coffee, juice, fruit and cheese - Ollie's usual leisurely breakfast, which they ate sitting at the window, revived them enough to talk.

"Not a one-night stand, after all, Ollie," said Charlotte.

"Two nights and three mornings, Lot darling, if anyone's counting," he replied.

"So what does that make us, Ollie love - an item, co-habs, de facs, common law spouses, partners?" she asked affectionately.

"Definitely not partners, unless we set up in practice together, and I hate the rest - a couple or significant others might do but there must be an acceptable description, let me think about it. Can't be fiancées, of course, since an engagement with anyone already married would be legally void on grounds of public policy. In the meantime, Lot darling, would you care to be called my consort?"

"Sort of Princess Albert you mean, to your King Victorious? I don't think so, darling. Why not just lovers?"

"Why not, indeed, we can write the ante-nuptial small print later," said Ollie, starting to clear the table. "More coffee, lover-girl?"

They reached the office before lunch, but not much before, having purchased sandwiches from the Southampton Row 'Upper Crust' on the way - actually bacon and egg baguettes in lieu of a traditional breakfast. No sign of Chair Frances nor of Sarah or Robin. Mrs Arden manned reception with undisguised disapproval of late arrivals. Maddie greeted Charlotte with none too subtle glee:

"At it again you two, eh?"

"None of your business - anyway you're only jealous."

"Jealous? I've nothing to be jealous about Lottie. Last evening my broker friend made a proposal to me!"

"What, marriage?" Charlotte exclaimed.

"No no not that, I wouldn't want to be married again, you bloody fool! No, he's going to their New York associates for six months and wants me to go too."

"In what capacity?"

"That's exactly what I asked. He said 'personal assistant etc.' Then he added the magic words: 'all expenses paid plus appropriate remuneration and prospects'!" hooted Maddie.

"So you're going, then," Charlotte concluded.

"You bet your sweet life Lottie - working here can be fun but not working there sounds more fun!"

"How old is he?"

"Oh don't be such a sad bag. A man's as old as he feels - he often says so," Maddie laughed at herself. "Actually he's bloody old, 64 next birthday, nearly a pensioner. But I won't mind that, not once I've got him to alter his will in my favour!"

Ollie entered cup in hand.

Chapter Twenty-Two

"Any left?" he asked.

"Might be stewed," said Maddie, fetching the coffee jug. "But you look as though you were too, Prof. What did you and Lot get up to last night?"

"Maddie's leaving us for six months in America," Charlotte intervened, shaking her head slightly at Ollie.

"Oh dear, not again," said he, sighing exaggeratedly. "Me know why, when?"

"End of the month and I may not be back this time!"

"We may not be here if you do come back," said Ollie a bit ambiguously. "Anyway you'll still be here for the wedding of the year. Robin's just rung to remind us: to-morrow 11.00 am precisely at Kensington Register Office in the old Chelsea Town Hall and afterwards in his flat off the Brompton Road. He doesn't think anyone from either his or Sarah's family will come after all - none have accepted - and they haven't invited any other friends or enemies. So they're banking on us - two to be witnesses. I'd already arranged delivery of a crate of Champagne to his flat, so at a bottle and a half each it should be a lively wedding breakfast!"

"I'll tell Chip and Mount - should we organise flowers from the office?" asked Maddie, distracted into action.

"Mrs Arden's already done that, but we could think of some more lasting gift, if petty cash will run to it!"

Ollie exited with his stewed coffee. Maddie bounced out to inform and consult. Charlotte brewed fresh coffee. Maddie returned with a gift idea: an Italian machine producing espresso and cappuccino for two. The idea was endorsed and, being beyond the resources of petty cash, she made a collection, Ollie funding a small deficit, and departed to acquire their gift.

Left in peace, Charlotte tried to work on the day's post, but concentration nonetheless proved elusive. She was relieved, therefore, when Ollie returned, an hour or so later, empty cup in hand.

"Lot, come and eat your baguette with me - I've something to show you."

They took their coffees and her baguette back down the corridor to Ollie's office, passing Mrs Arden who grimaced at them. Could that have been a smile through tears? wondered Charlotte. Ollie closed the door, gesturing to her to sit down. First he showed her two hand-written, barely legible, letters of resignation, as of Friday the Thirteenth of April, 1989. No reason given except that he was unwilling to continue as Ombudsman. One was addressed to BIG's Bob, the other to Frankie Freeman, Council Chairman, c/o Robin Wood, Council Clerk, both at the Ombudsman's office.

"Didn't get Mrs Arden to type them 'cause I'd rather tell people myself to-morrow, after the wedding."

"But is that enough, sending them here?" Charlotte asked.

"Should be, I've checked the rules. But I'll also send copies by special courier, just in case. And I've thoughtfully drafted an advert for my replacement - what do you think?"

Ollie showed Charlotte another piece of paper, this time typed. She read it:

"BIG INSURANCE OMBUDSMAN -(c £50K, no benefits)

Chapter Twenty-Two

The Insurance Ombudsman Scheme (IOS) is a private, voluntary undertaking belonging to the British Insurance Group (BIG). The IOS's business mission is to counter press perceptions that all insurers act as prosecutor, judge and jury, prejudicially to legitimate claims. BIG funds the IOS out of policyholders' premiums in order to provide an ostensibly independent conciliation and adjudication arrangement capable of reassuring politicians otherwise inclined towards non-self regulatory legislation.

With the approval of BIG's Board of Directors, applications are invited for the pressurised appointment of Ombudsman, which has just been relinquished by the present incumbent after a short struggle. The ideal candidate may possibly possess formal legal qualifications, which should not necessarily be an insurmountable handicap provided he or she does not enjoy any insurance expertise or consumerist experience. She or he will welcome the intellectual stimulus of concentrating on the IOS's core product - rehandling rejected claims under household and motor policies (particularly as to deteriorating flat felt roofs and second-hand values of written-off cars). Communication skills must be prioritised so that policyholders can properly understand not only the altruistic integrity of the insurance industry but also its public duty to identify and terminate fraudulent and vexatious claimants.

The appointment is for a probationary period of two years and falls outside the Employment Protection legislation. Reappointment is a possibility, provided personally favourable publicity has been avoided and subject to non-professional performance appraisal by the Chair (sic) reporting to variably informed and occasionally interested Council Members. A satisfactory track record of conciliatory attendance at Council coffee mornings whilst respectfully treating the Chair as if coherent, and submitting to her prepared speeches without interruption or obvious embarrassment, will be appraised as a paramount probationary factor.

Applications, marked for administrative convenience non-confidential, should be addressed to Ms Frankie Freeman, 'Chair (sic)' of Council, c/o Personnel Manager, British Insurance Group, Bournemouth, England, the World."

Finishing reading Charlotte looked at a hovering Ollie, who looked pleased with himself.

"Well, what do you think?" he asked, smirking.

"Tear it up, you twerp," she advised. "I'm leaving now to learn the worst about the boys - find out whether mother's still surviving. May ring later, but otherwise see you at the church, sorry registry office, to-morrow - eleven o'clock on the dot!"

She left him smirkless and, for once, speechless.

Chapter Twenty-Three

Final Friday

Friday the thirteenth, fifteen minutes before due dot time, Ollie and all his Assistants had assembled in the Kensington Registry office waiting-room. A grimly tearful Mrs Arden was also there. Apart from a familiar corduroy suit, smart dress was the order of the day, topped off for every single one of Ollie's ladies, even Mount, by a broad-brimmed hat. Charlotte had not rung him the night before, but had arrived at his flat that morning just to share his usual breakfast - she had kept her smart kit on. Nevertheless tears escaped from her big green eyes: the imponderables of marriage and the emotions of lovers found relief in crying. Ollie held her closely and comfortingly, once again speechless.

At ten to eleven, Robin hurried in, alone and looking worried. Where was Sarah? And no moustache!

"What's up with your gob?" cried Maddie. "Where's your toothbrush gone?"

"She'd only marry me if I shaved it off," Robin said, a touch shamefacedly Charlotte thought.

Five minutes later, the Registrar's Assistant, a beautiful black woman, poked her head round the door.

"Mr Wood?" she enquired. "Phone call for you."

Robin followed her.

With one minute to go he returned to the waiting-room, still alone but no longer looking worried.

"She's called it off!" he announced loudly.

"Oh you poor sod," screamed Maddie. "Jilted at the altar!"

"Alternative altar," Ollie murmured but Charlotte, observing that Robin looked a little less than upset, asked gently:

"Do you mind?"

"No, not at all, nor does she - she's not pregnant after all you see! Means we don't have to get married now but can go on as we are. What a bloody relief!"

"You're not splitting up?" Chip's voice was shrilly incredulous.

"Absolutely not - she's moved in with me anyway, I've told her to go straight back to the flat."

Robin paused, evidently remembering the pre-arranged wedding celebrations involving a delivered gift and a crate of champagne. He continued:

"What do you say to all coming to the flat anyway? The Prof's bubbly's mostly on ice and tell the truth I feel over the moon, much more like bloody celebrating than I would of as a poor bloody hubby-man!"

His English language was lapsing with the marital weight removed.

"Talking of moons," Charlotte ventured. "Is there honey still for tea?"

"What d'you mean?" demanded Robin.

"The honeymoon. . ."

". . . BIG's travel policy won't cover cancellation!" shrieked Maddie.

"Oh, I don't know, have to see what Sarah says - but if we're going to lose money, we'll probably go anyway, never been to Jamaica and I'm told it's hot there!"

Charlotte saw that the leer had returned and thought it slightly less offensive without the moustache.

In the event, they did all follow Robin back to his flat, except for Mrs Arden who took her departure without a word but with grim disapproval all over her face. First floor back of a post-war block, living-room, kitchen, bath/WC and two bedrooms, it was much bigger than Ollie's flat and also poshly situated.

"How'd you get this then?" demanded Maddie. "Must have cost a fortune!"

"No, I'm a Rent Act tenant," explained Robin. "Landlord's a charity, supposed to let to poor old people, but they only get single women - widows mostly - and flats like this are too big for one occupier. Not allowed to sell so they have to let to other deserving paupers, usually employees of their solicitors or property agents - or their friends and Sarah can be very friendly, know what I mean?" He was leering again.

The flat was furnished as if by someone who had just moved from smaller accommodation, which Robin said he had. Some of his toy soldiers were on display - Charlotte observed with interest the tableau, Freudian perhaps, of a Court Martial. However happily the furnishings included that day's essentials: a large fridge filled with bottles of champagne and a dining-table bearing a big oval platter of smoked salmon sandwiches, still wrapped in cellophane. Ordered and delivered that morning, according to Robin who began to unwrap the sandwiches. Ollie had already assumed the role of butler or barman and was opening and pouring the champagne, but not with skill Charlotte noticed, thinking his expertise derives from drinking rather than serving. She passed the glasses round, remarking to Robin:

"Lucky none of your families came, in the circumstances."

"No luck about it," he replied, "they weren't invited - my lot don't like her and her lot can't stand me."

"Didn't you invite any other friends either?" asked Chip.

"We don't have any friends in common, so we didn't tell them. Hers are all horsey and she doesn't want them to know about me and mine are all from the YMCA and I definitely don't want them knowing about Sarah - for one thing they think I'm gay, some of them with cause."

Robin's leer seemed somewhat strained.

Sarah herself arrived at the flat nearly an hour later in a taxi with several suitcases. Robin and Mount carried them up. Ollie offered to help but Mount pushed him away:

"Get off Prof - I'm stronger than you, and steadier on my feet, pour Sarah a drink instead."

"Alright," said Ollie and, after the cases had been carried up and everybody's glass filled, continued:

"If Robin and Sarah could be prised apart for a moment - thank you - I'd like us all to drink a toast to their happiness. Itemhood, aka cohabitation, is a not dishonourable estate, but one esteemed by many in high places and which should not be - and I know is not - undertaken lightly. But I don't see why it should be undertaken soberly. To Sarah and Robin, everybody's

Chapter Twenty-Three

heartiest congratulations!"

They all drank, then smilingly said all sorts of supportive somethings. Everyone kissed Sarah and everyone bar Ollie kissed Robin. Maddie reminded them that the coffee machine came from all of them and, like a pet, could be a friend for life although tending to attract other drinkers.

Ollie opened another bottle and refilled all their glasses, before calling for quiet and announcing:

"I've not finished yet. Not a speech but two pieces of news. First the good news, which may or may not come as a surprise to some of you. Itemhood has also struck Lottie and me!"

"About time you went public," crowed Maddie.

"Yeah, she's had to tell us all in confidence," said Chip.

"You know, one at a time," added Mount.

"Here's to the Prof and Lottie," cried Robin.

"Welcome to the club," Sarah simpered.

They all drank again and Ollie continued:

"As to the club, I've been doing some research to find an appropriate and acceptable word to call people in our happy but unwed situation. Can't introduce Lottie as 'my item'. And the answer is a 'leman'!"

"A lemon, you clown?" laughed Charlotte, while the rest awaited, a little in trepidation, to hear a lapsed academic's joke, wondering whether they would understand it when it came.

"Or do you mean a lemming?"

"No, leman, spelt with an 'a' not an 'o'", he replied extracting a slip of paper from his wallet. "Listen to

249

the Concise OED definition: '*leman n (pl lemans)* 1 a lover or sweetheart 2 an illicit lover, esp. a mistress'. So, ladies and gentleman, I'm pleased to announce that Lot has consented to become 'my leman'. Of course if wee Frankie Free, the Chair were here, God forbid, I'd have to say 'my le'."

He pronounced it 'luh', but continued: "Or more accurately in every sense 'my lay'!"

"Let me see that," cried Charlotte snatching the slip of paper. "I thought so - it also says 'archaic'."

"Well I am older than you, Lot, I mean Lottie, darling one."

"But I do like the Middle English version," she continued: "'*leofman*' - presumably pronounced half-way between 'leaf' and 'love'. So everyone, meet 'my leoffer'." She made it sound more like 'loafer' than 'lover' which at least amused the rest.

"What about 'toy-girl' and 'toe-rag'," shouted Maddie, or perhaps it was the champagne.

"And now for the bad news," Ollie was going to spoil the party.

"This may come as a bit of a bombshell from the blue, but I have resigned as Ombudsman with effect from high noon to-day. To escape the curse of Council. My Lottie has also given notice, but not for the same reason. I've absolutely no idea what will happen to the office but I'm not optimistic."

This announcement produced a shocked silence. Until Maddie began to sing sadly:

"Ollie the Ombudsman packed his trunk
And said good-bye to the circus."

Chapter Twenty-Three

Whilst Charlotte held his hand and quietly wept.

THE END
(Of The Beginning. . .?)

Love At All Risks